WHIP IT

WHIP IT

Shauna Cross

SQUARE
FISH

Henry Holt and Company
New York

Special thanks to Mom, Dad, the fam, Steven Malk, Kiwi Smith, Seth Jaret, Jason Lust, Fred Jasper, Frank Portman, Jonathan Hennessey and the Soly Gang.

An Imprint of Macmillan

Library of Congress Cataloging-in-Publication Data
Cross, Shauna.
Derby girl / Shauna Cross.
p.   cm.
Summary: When sixteen-year-old rebel Bliss Cavendar, who is miserable living in a small Texas town with her beauty pageant-obsessed mother, secretly joins a roller derby team under the name "Babe Ruthless," her life gets better, although infinitely more confusing.
ISBN: 978-0-312-53599-5
[1. Roller derbies—Fiction.   2. Identity—Fiction.   3. Interpersonal relations—Fiction.   4. High schools—Fiction.   5. Schools—Fiction.   6. Texas—Fiction.]
I. Title.
PZ7.C88275De 2007   [Fic]—dc22   2006036357

Originally published in the United States by Henry Holt and Company under the title *Derby Girl*
Square Fish logo designed by Filomena Tuosto
Designed by Amelia May Anderson
First Square Fish Edition: 2009
10 9 8 7 6 5 4
www.squarefishbooks.com

To any & all misfit girls,
this one's for you.

WHIP IT

The Not-So-Sweet Life

I don't know how it happened or what sort of back-room deal went down, but apparently I'm living in a small Texas town with two culturally clueless impostors for legal guardians, when I just know my real parents are out there somewhere. They're probably these super-cool artist types with a loft in New York. Or maybe they're in San Francisco. That would work too. I'd take San Fran over this cow-patty town any day.

Dear Potentially Cool Parental Folk,
If you suddenly realize you're
missing one charmingly sarcastic

16-year-old daughter, send a plane
ticket. I'm ready to come home.
                XO,
                Your Forgiving Offspring
    P.S. If you aren't my real
parents and you happen to find
this note (and you are hip and
childless), I urge you to consider
the wonderful world of adoption.*
    * Adoption offer good only for
those living in a cool city. Cool
city to be determined by adoptee.

2

I wrote that on a note card last spring when I was
forced to participate in an oh-so-lame balloon release
at school (don't ask). So far, I've had exactly zero
responses, but I'm keepin' hope alive.

Hope is pretty much the only way to survive Bodeen,
Texas. Unless, of course, you're a football-throwing,
truck-worshipping, country-music-listening hick. Then,
naturally, Bodeen is your soul mate of a town. Yay, you.

But if you happen to be an indie-rock-loving, thrift-
store-prowling, homemade-T-shirt-wearing, blue-hair-
dying misfit girl who thinks life is a '60s movie, then
Bodeen can be, and often is, one giant ball of suck.

Ah, beautiful Bodeen, home of the unironic mullet
and the "world-famous" Bluebonnet ice cream factory.

The frozen yum-yums are produced locally, and people travel far and wide just to get a glimpse of the ice cream makin' in action. Honestly, the process is about as riveting as golf on Saturday TV, but the tourists *ooh* and *ahh* like it's a freakin' religious experience, like the rocky road they're munching on isn't the exact same crap they can buy by the gallon at their local Piggly Wiggly.

By the way, when I say tourists, I don't mean to imply Bodeen is a mecca for world travelers or anyone remotely interesting, i.e., crushworthy boys. The whole ice-cream-factory-as-vacation-destination thing doesn't really speak to that demographic. Believe me, I have done my research on this one. I have spent countless hours watching tour bus after tour bus unload, desperately hoping for a glimpse of male cuteness among the fat-ass, fanny-pack parade—it never happens. You will see Jesus skateboarding the streets of Bodeen before a hot guy ever wanders across the county line.

And if that isn't enough, Bodeen has somehow become synonymous with "romantic getaway for two," which means other people's parents drag their sad relationships out here for a little weekend "rekindling." They check into one of our *charming* bed and breakfasts and get busy doing whatever it is parent folk do when surrounded by grandma wallpaper, doily curtains, and the scent of fresh-baked muffins (cringe factor high!).

Every Friday night, when these couples descend on

my little town, I think, *Somewhere scattered across Texas are a bunch of teenage boys whose parents left them alone for the weekend.* And I think there must be one boy, one witty, music-obsessed cutie, who could really appreciate a girl with blue hair and an impressive CD collection . . . and I think, *Why aren't I with him? I SHOULD BE THERE WHILE HIS PARENTS ARE HERE.*

It hurts. It really does.

Little House on the Scary

So, you might as well know my name is Bliss Cavendar. God, just saying it out loud makes me want to hurl. The Bliss part is particularly cruel, considering I haven't experienced any (unless you count my banana Laffy Taffy obsession—but that only takes a girl so far). Obviously, my nutso mother was expecting a tap-dancing ray of sunshine when she was shopping for baby names. Instead, she got me. Surprise. No tap dancing, no sunshine.

To make matters worse, Brooke (my alleged real mother) suffers from a rare but raging illness: addiction to beauty pageants. Tiara-ism, I like to call it. Apparently Brooke was a major hottie back in her day, winning a slew of titles, crowns, and sashes, including the local end-all, be-all crown, Miss Bluebonnet. My grandmother and great-grandmother were also Miss Bluebonnets.

Unfortunately for Brooke, Miss Bluebonnet wasn't enough. She hungered for, but never quite made it to, the pageant big leagues, a fact that has fueled her epic, *Lord of the Rings* style quest to ensure that her child wins the ultimate crown. Yep, Brooke decided that if she couldn't be a Miss America herself, she would be the proud mother of a Miss America. That's where I come in, victim #1.

I spent my formative years participating in one rhinestone torture-a-thon after another (I was so naive then). Brooke would tease my stringy hair skyscraper high and spackle on so much makeup that, I swear to God, you could see it on satellite photos from space. I never won anything more than "Certificate of Participation," which is pageant-speak for "big-ass loser."

But that didn't stop Brooke, who does not let little things like reality get in her way when she is doggedly pursuing a goal. She hooked me up with a coach, and on my thirteenth birthday, I debuted a new talent routine that was supposed to propel me to the title of "Little Miss Howdy-Roo" in the nearby town of Dripping Springs.

Ladies and Gentlemen: Y'all give a big Texas welcome to Bliss Cavendar, baton-twirling sensation!

You have to believe me when I tell you I gave that damn baton everything I had. I twirled, whirled, and step-ball-changed like my life depended on it. But the hairspray made me dizzy, and somewhere in the middle of my showstopping finale, the choreography gods took a smoke break and left me hangin'. The baton ricocheted off my cartwheeling foot, sailed into the audience, and coldcocked judge Darla Schaffer right upside the head. Well, you can't say it wasn't a showstopper. It took Mrs. Schaffer five minutes to regain consciousness.

On the rainy drive home, as I clutched yet another "Certificate of Participation," Mom kept saying, "It's okay, sugar. We just gotta nail that finale and we're golden. You don't get to be Miss America by giving up, you know." But I did know, and I was over it. Two weeks later, I launched a Gandhi-inspired hunger strike and finally secured freedom from my mother's pageant cult. Sort of.

She still expects me to compete in Miss Bluebonnet in December—a painful fact I try to keep buried way, way in the back of my mind. I consider it the final stop on my long and completely unsuccessful pageant train ride.

Meanwhile, Mom turned her Miss America sights on my little sister, Shania (another bad but very pageant-friendly name), who just turned . . . drumroll please . . . four years old. I call my angelic little sis Sweet Pea because I find her Brooke-given name too repugnant to utter out loud. Plus, when Sweet Pea grows up and looks back on her childhood, I want her to know I was fighting the good fight on her behalf.

The strange thing about Sweet Pea, the four-year-old pageant queen, is that she really seems to love competing. She never cries or threatens to run away when Brooke teases her hair. And, get this, the kid actually squeals with delight when she gets to wear that abominable piece of bedazzled cotton candy pretending to be a dress. Maybe that's why she always wins. She's Brooke's pageant dream come true.

Sometimes I feel guilty, like I should be protecting Sweet Pea from my mom's cult (being a survivor, and all). But, at the same time, I'm grateful because my little sis brings home the trophy bacon like I never could, which keeps Brooke off my back. And my motto is, the less Brooke in my life, the better.

Of course this JC Penney family portrait wouldn't be complete without mentioning my pa, Earl Cavendar. Here's all you need to know about good ol' Earl. The Cliffs Notes if you will. He owns Longhorn Furniture (home of the world's ugliest sofas), says maybe three words a day, and usually falls asleep in his maroon velour ("melour") La-Z-Boy after the football report. Earl knows he's no match for the Texas Twister he married and has adopted a cunning survival tactic: He does exactly what he's told and stays the hell out of Brooke's way.

Oh, and here's a fun fact. I recently discovered that, contrary to official family records, Earl and Brooke's *actual* wedding date is only five months before my birthday. Surprise, surprise. Ain't true love grand?

The Pash Amini Show

*D*espite the staggering odds against me, I have managed to find the best friend a small-town weirdo girl like me could ever hope for: the one, the only, Pash Amini. Last year, when I was dying from boredom (I'm talkin' ICU—it did not look good), Pash moved to town and nursed me back to social health.

She wasn't in the school forty-five minutes before she hunted me down at my locker. She fearlessly approached, tossing all new-girl-in-school rules blithely to the side.

"Hey," she said, "my name's Pash, as in *passion*."

I took one look at her '50s pencil skirt and homemade skull earrings while she silently graded my tuxedo-striped Dickies and '70s "Hopscotch for Jesus" T-shirt. It was best friend love at first sight.

Not only is she hilarious and crazy smart (straight As, honors everything), but Pash is the most beautiful Arab-American bombshell this side of the Pecos River. The *only* Arab-American bombshell, she would remind me. Naturally, Pash's exotic gorgeousness has yet to receive the props it deserves from the knuckle-dragging idiots at Bodeen High. I know her pain. Not that there are any lads worth swooning over, but it would be nice to be admired. Secretly admired, even.

It's the height of summer and a thousand and two degrees in the blistering August heat, just a friendly reminder that Bodeen, Texas, really is hell. Pash and I wander through town enjoying our last half hour of freedom before we clock in at The Job So Awful We Dare Not Speak Its Name (TJSAWDNSIN).

Okay, I'm going to explain this once and once only. Then, you should swallow this piece of paper because I was never here. Pash and I work at the Oink Joint, a barbecue restaurant "famous" (i.e., not famous at all) for the giant, two-story pig sculpture that sits in the parking lot, the most tourist-trappy of tourist traps.

TJSAWDNSIN is so awful that I was holding out for a job at Wal-Mart before I took it. It's the place you go when no one else will have you. Naturally, Pash and I were shoo-ins.

We share a double-dip Bluebonnet waffle cone of cookies and cream (me) and mint chocolate chip (her), sword fighting with our plastic spoons. Now, as much as I detest the tacky tourist trade that has sprung up around the Bluebonnet factory, I'd be lying if I didn't admit that their ice cream is my most beloved food group. Those Bodeen dairy cows have got some serious skill.

I could, however, do without the Bluebonnet ads that dot the town landscape. You can't walk two blocks without having a billboard shoved in your face, and not just any billboard. The Bluebonnet billboards are a cultural phenom unto themselves. They always feature the reigning Miss Bluebonnet in a cleavage-baring milkmaid costume, smiling as she licks a glistening ice cream cone. Sexy, yet wholesome (so as not to cast doubt on Miss Bluebonnet's chastity, this being a Christian community, and all).

Now, you-know-who cannot pass a billboard without sighing dramatically, "That's your destiny, Bliss," which only happens about . . . thirty-five times a day. Give or take.

The current competition for the Miss Bluebonnet crown is Corbi Booth, varsity cheerleader and a real chipmunk of a girl. Frankly, I'd just hand her the crown today if it wouldn't send Brooke into a tailspin. Corbi and I were best friends (*BFF!*) a million years ago, but when I discovered real music and she devoted her life to the pursuit of the perfect lip gloss, it was time to go our separate ways.

Now, you know and I know, and everyone in the whole free world knows, that come December Corbi will get the crown and I'll fade into pageant obscurity, but there's a little hitch. Corbi's mom, Val, a poster woman for all things plastic, still sees me as stiff competition because of my impressive Miss Bluebonnet lineage. Oh, and the fact that my mom kicked her ass the year she won.

So, no matter how much of a dark horse I seem— c'mon, a girl with blue hair?—I'm persona non grata on Corbi's bitch-o-meter.

What Corbi lacks in intelligence she makes up for in catty gossip and tiny skirts. She also happens to be the longtime girlfriend of Bodeen High's star quarterback, Colby Miller. Colby and Corbi—awwww, isn't that so cute? (Answer: not cute *at all!*)

The whole town is under some sort of twisted assumption that this cliché masquerading as a sweeping high school romance is Bodeen's answer to a Hollywood couple. They can't get enough of the adorable twosome.

But Pash and I have had more than our fill, thankyou-verymuch. We can't even enjoy our ice cream without the dynamic duo suddenly appearing out of nowhere in

Colby's my-dad-bought-me-this-ginormous-pickup-truck-because-I-am-a-football-god mobile with his future Miss Bluebonnet nestled at his side as "Brooks & Dumb" blares out the windows (the cherry on this little torture sundae).

And what is it with teenagers who have perfect zitfree skin right in the middle of what is supposed to be the zittiest time in their lives? It is beyond unfair. Surely there will be some payback later in life for that . . . or there is no justice.

The lovebirds stop at a red light, and Colby glances at us—at me, actually. His face contorts with contempt and confusion, like, *How the hell are you even allowed to exist?* Corbi shudders and clutches Colby's steroid-inflated biceps, as if to say, *Get me out of here before their weirdness totally rubs off on me!* (Like I'm not the girl whose bed she used to pee in when she spent the night at my house—how dare she judge me?)

The second the light turns green, Colby and Corbi speed away like terrified teen lovers fleeing a pack of hungry zombies in a trashy horror flick. I never knew I was so scary. I almost take it as a compliment.

Pash and I are silent as the hot Tejas air hangs between us. We are both thinking the same depressing thought, so there's no point in actually saying it out loud. *How come those idiots can find love when we have to suffer a romance drought?* But Pash can't keep her mouth shut for long. It's physically impossible, medically documented.

"Bliss, I know my New Year's resolution was not to obsess, but if I don't get some serious boy-on-Pash action stat, I'm gonna explode," she says.

"Then people really will think you're a terrorist," I offer, and Pash cracks up. Yes, racism is alive and well in Bodeen, and my girl has suffered her share of slurs and suspicious stares, so we mock the hillbillies any chance we get. Dark humor rules.

Le Joint d'Oink

$\mathscr{I}$ could go on and on about the horror of facing the public in a heinous gingham smock, the constant stench of barbecue in my hair, and the soul-sucking task of timing unhealthy people as they try to eat the Squealer Sandwich (ten pounds of pulled pork) in ten minutes so that they can win a free T-shirt and have their picture placed on the "Squeal of Fame."

But really, it's not so bad as long as Pash and I have the same schedule.

We amuse ourselves by constantly rebelling against the Oink Joint system. It also helps that Dwayne "Bird-man" Johnston is totally in love with both of us. Not that that's flattering in any way, shape, or form. Trust me. Bird-man is all geek, all the time, and not of the chic variety. Although he's kind of been on a power trip since they officially promoted him to manager.

Like today. Pash and I were up to our old survival tricks, taking some brilliantly funny pictures (if I do say so myself), then covertly posting them on the "Squeal of Fame" billboard among all the yellowed snapshots of fat tourists holding up clean plates. Bird-man comes flying from across the restaurant waving his skinny arms.

"What do you two think you're doing?" he said, cornering us and trying to sound authoritative, as though he'd been hiding out in the back, practicing his manager voice.

"Creating art," Pash explained, pointing to a Polaroid of me staring down at a trash-can-sized vat of barbecue sauce. "It's called 'Girl Contemplates Killing Herself in the Secret Sauce.'"

"A very important piece, Bird-man," I added. He tried to make us take it down, but after we ridiculed him for going corporate, he agreed to let the artwork stay for a week.

"And," he added, "I want you guys to start calling me Dwayne now that I'm manager. It's more dignified."

"No way," Pash protested. "Bird-man is way sexier."

"Yeah, it gives you an air of mystery," I added as we walked away.

Thus, Bird-man agreed to keep going by Bird-man. It's really the only thing he has going for him; we couldn't let him screw that up. It's little triumphs like that that make TJSAWDNSIN bearable. That, and the Pash Amini / Bliss Cavendar closing routine.

Pash will be mopping and suddenly throw me that wicked smile she gets right before breaking into song. We have this game where we pretend our job is a really bad musical. We make up our own lyrics to Broadway tunes, giving the classics a little Pashification.

Today it's "Over the Rainbow" sung at a more youth-friendly punk rock tempo. Take it away, Pash.

> *Somewhere over the rainbow, Bliss's hair is blue,*
> *There's a land that I heard of once, full of*
>   *yummy guys!*
> *Someday I'll meet a boy who plays no sports,*
> *He'll want me for my brilliant mind and not*
>   *Cause I wear booty shorts,*
> *In his bed—that's where you'll fiiiiiind me!*

We bust out some hilariously bad dance moves that will never see the light of MTV, pausing dramatically for our bigger-than-big finish.

> *Somewhere over the rainbow, blue birds play,*
> *If blue birds play,*
> *Then why can't we get laid?*

Pash, who's, like, half my size, dips me, and we collapse into a booth like a laughing house of cards. I'm not sure if the genius of this spontaneous musical moment translates, but believe me, we could take this show on the road. Or maybe we're high from the smell of slow-cooked meat.

As we lock up and bid Bird-man adieu, I look up at the Miss Bluebonnet billboard across the street. "God. If I don't get away from these, this town is going to see my wrath."

"Oh, really?" Pash raises a single eyebrow with devious super-villain precision. "Is someone feeling . . . criminal?"

"Oh, Ms. Amini, I thought you'd never ask," I say in my best Scarlett O'Hara voice as we link arms and head off for some good ol'-fashioned trouble. Yeehaw.

19

Hootenanny on Aisle Seven

*I*t's not like I'm ga-ga in love with shoplifting. I only do it to keep my mind off more devious activities, like cheerleading and prom planning. Plus, Wal-Mart is so totally asking for it with the crappy way they treat their workers. And I'm not just saying that because they wouldn't hire me (they had "issues" with my wardrobe—whatev). Who the hell wants to work at Wal-Mart, anyway? The polyester smocks are a total identity killer.

The gigantic doors slide open, and the store welcomes Pash and me with an air-conditioned embrace. We scout the aisles for five-finger-discount inspiration. I seductively wave a Toby Keith CD at Pash.

"Your boyfriend says hi."

"Friends don't let friends listen to Toby Keith," Pash declares, snatching the offending music out of my hand and burying it under a pile of White Stripes CDs.

We mosey over to the lingerie department and giggle past the racks of monster granny panties (immature, yes, but hilarious nonetheless).

"Think of all the elastic that had to die just to make these panties," Pash says sadly.

We press on, refusing to let the granny-brief grief derail our mission. Pash and I stumble into an abandoned, messy dressing room with our covert picks behind our backs.

"You first," she insists, and I hold up a hooker-red bra with gold lace in exactly Pash's size.

"You really hate me!" she squeals before producing a hot-pink leopard-print bra for me.

"Back at ya." I laugh as we try on our tacky bras. I look over at Pash. Life is cruel. Her boobs are hall-of-fame perfect, even in a cheap, ugly bra.

"Oh, that is so not fair!" I say. "I picked the nastiest one, and it still looks amazing on you!"

"Yeah, well, I'd trade my boobs for your perfect flat stomach any day," she counters, which makes me feel slightly better about my less-than-ample cup size.

Plus, the leopard bra is actually kinda cute on me. Sort of a retro Marilyn Monroe sex-bomb thing, only I'm not Marilyn Monroe, nor am I a sex bomb. But on the off chance I morph into such a creature, it's comforting to know I'll have the right bra standing by.

Minutes later, Pash and I exit the dressing room with our garish new lingerie safely stowed beneath our grubby T-shirts. We do a couple of casual laps around the store so as not to arouse suspicion.

That is, until Pash points out a black globe hiding a security camera in the gun section—technically, the "sportsman department." *If shooting a gun is a sport,* I think, *then so is stealing a bra. I'm going to lobby the Olympic Committee to recognize my sport, petition for some sponsors. Gold medal, bra-thieving victory here I come.*

"Hey, I don't think their stupid security cameras even work," Pash says.

"Really? Why don't you flash them and find out?" I taunt her, forgetting that Pash will happily perform any half dare thrown her way. Which usually means I'll have to perform it too, part of the unspoken best-friend manifesto.

True to form, she's got her T-shirt hiked up in mock Girls Gone Wild stance before I yank it down like an uptight parent trying to keep her three-year-old daughter from flashing her panties on the playground.

"We're leaving," I say, grabbing her wrist.

"Sure thing. *After* you give a little love to the spy cam," she insists. Pash follows her command with a look that says, *We're in this together,* guilting me from letting her take the potential fall for both of us.

So, like lightning on the prairie, I flash with quickie speed. T-shirt up, T-shirt down. Now, let's get the hell out of here.

We stroll toward the exit and sweetly wave good-bye to the eighty-year-old lady workin' the door (apparently, *she's* allowed to have blue hair, but I am not).

When we cross the parking lot, Pash and I are home free. Wal-Mart never knew what hit 'em.

Back to Fool Shopping

*O*kay, I don't know which saint to salute or god to bow down to, but I just witnessed a minor miracle in my very own bedroom. Brooke actually knocked on my door (a shocker in its own right), and upon gaining entry, she offered to take me to Austin to get some school clothes. Austin! (Angels sing, clouds part, sun shines down, and I am skipping through fields of daisies.)

You must understand that, compared to Bodeen, Austin is New York City. Anything cool that happens in Texas happens in Austin, end of story. You see, Austin has this thing that Bodeen doesn't: It's called "civilization." Cool movie theaters, stores you're not ashamed to shop at, and real music clubs! Not that crap like Ricky's I-10

Roadhouse, where rednecks go to "boot-scoot-boogie," but real places where indie and punk bands play live music *every night*. If Austin were some standardized test question, it would go something like this:

Cool is to NYC as _____ is to Texas.
Answer: Austin.

Austin is only an hour's drive from Bodeen, but it's a "whole 'nother world," as they say. Since I have yet to procure my own vehicle (Pash and I are working on it, trust me), my only chance of leaving town is in *la limousine de Brooke*. I take her up on her offer *tout de suite*.

I am so crazy excited, I ignore all the warning signs that suggest this wave of Oprah-inspired, mother/daughter love just might come crashing down on the shores of reality.

Warning sign #1: Pash is not allowed to come with, which usually guarantees good Brooke behavior. Now I'm on my own without my best-friend protective shield.

Warning sign #2: Contrary to the just-us sales pitch, my mom suddenly insists Sweet Pea tag along so she too can get some new clothes (her pint-sized wardrobe is already twice the size of mine). This means there will be a Disney Store excursion, and it is against my beliefs to step foot in a Disney Store.

Warning sign #3: Brooke seems to be ignoring my

meticulously researched Internet data concerning the best places to shop—i.e., near the university, the epicenter of cool.

But none of this squelches my excitement. On the drive up, I am perfect. I don't even flinch when Brooke tosses my Hot Hot Heat CD in the backseat to make way for her Céline Dion sing-along with Sweet Pea. My Stepford-daughter performance is so convincing that I wonder if I am in fact a great undiscovered actress. I picture myself winning an Academy Award and giving a speech so brilliant it inspires misfit girls everywhere to rise up against their oppressors. I am a one-woman revolution.

But two hours later in a crummy suburban mall, my façade is beginning to crack. For Brooke to pay for my clothes, Brooke has to approve of my clothes, which requires careful diplomacy. She hates everything I like, and I hate everything she likes. There is no middle ground.

Why can't I be one of those kids whose parents just let them take the credit card and get what they want without interference? Somebody please fill me in on the magic potion that gets your parents to obey these laws of teen shopping.

The more I withdraw, the more Brooke pushes. Pink, pink, and more pink. At one point she even holds up a pair of jeans with pink suede fringe running down the legs (!) and dares to ask why I don't like them. Seriously, if there were a Smithsonian exhibit of America's butt-ugliest

jeans, these would be the pièce de résistance. And she wants me to tell her what's wrong with them?

"Um, everything," I say.

"Well, that's your opinion," she snaps, all offended.

"I think they're just darlin'. They'd be great for Shania's new cowgirl talent routine. I'm gonna get them for costume inspiration.

Oh, pardon me, I had this whole day wrong. I thought we were back-to-school shopping for Bliss, but apparently we're pageant shopping for Shania. I didn't get that memo.

We head to the Gap, aka "the Crap" (b/c Pash and I find their version of cool a little too forced), but I can at least buy a couple of T-shirts to cut up and customize. I grab anything and everything, make a beeline for the dressing room, and treat myself to a much-needed break from Brooke.

I can hear my mom roaming the store making singsong chitchat with someone about "how difficult" I am to shop for. That two-faced cow. Excuse me, why should I have to take fashion advice from a forty-one-year-old who considers the Michaels craft store her house of couture?

In the mirror I discover a monster zit in the middle of my forehead. It looks like a baby horn. Lovely. On top of it all, I'm becoming a unicorn. I bite my tongue to keep myself from crying.

As we head for the car, I finally let my mom have it.

"Why can't I just go to one, one store that is not in a mall? One store where I might actually find something that I like? You promised me a trip to Austin. This isn't Austin, this is a suburban mall."

There is a long pause, like Brooke can barely comprehend what I'm saying, as if it never occurred to her to shop outside of a mall. At last she says, "Okay, Bliss, what is your idea of Austin?"

"Well, like, down by the college, where the noncorporate stores are. It's not even ten minutes away."

She gives me this martyr sigh, like I'm asking the impossible, like I expect her to carry me there on her back.

"Fine," she says. "One store."

"Awesome! Let's go to Atomic City. They have the best shoes!" I squeal, well aware that my mom is desperate to see me in something other than these busted Chuck Taylors with the silver duct tape around the toe (a fuck-off fashion do if there ever was one).

I enter Atomic City, a rambling store in an old house that caters to the local punks, rockabilly kids, goths, hippies, ravers, mods, and anyone else not represented by the mainstream. I practically sprint past the Manic Panic hair dye, the Japanime T-shirts, the kiosk of cooler-than-thou sunglasses, and retro pin-up dresses in search of what I came here for: John Fluevog shoes. And the selection is even better in person than what you see online. Score!

I try on several styles and gather opinions from a trio of to-die-for cute boys who are also shopping. They are way college-aged, and Brooke is in full spy mode, so I have to keep the flirting to a min. But trust me, I am swooning on the inside. Big time. I even forget (momentarily) about my unicorn zit. *This* is my kind of Austin.

I finally decide on a pair of chunky Mary-Janes in bright purple with two turquoise straps. Cool and comfy and worth every penny of the 175-dollar asking price (my entire back-to-school budget, plus some saved-up baby-sitting money). Best of all, this fab footwear says, to even the most casual of observers, "I was not purchased in a mall." Maybe on Mars, but definitely not in a mall.

Even Brooke seems relieved to be buying me something I obviously love. She is just about to slap down the plastic and seal the deal when something across the store catches her eye: a shelf of bright-colored glass illuminated by the late-afternoon sun.

"Ooh, now those are pretty!" she exclaims a little too loudly before realizing what it is she's admiring. It's a shelf of foot-long bongs.

My mother's face goes white, as everyone in Atomic City turns away and laughs their collective ass off.

Brooke is mor-ti-fied. It takes exactly three seconds for her to reconsider my prized purchase. "Bliss," she says, so piously I can practically see the halo hovering above her head, "I don't think I would be doing my job as a mother if I bought you your back-to-school shoes from an establishment that also sells drug paraphernalia. Do you?"

"Mom," I say, trying to calmly navigate the choppy waters of my mother's mood swing, "I just want the shoes, not the bong."

"First it's the shoes, then it's the bong."

"Yeah, right." I laugh. "Shoes are the gateway drug."

"Very funny, Bliss," she scoffs, not laughing. "Apparently you don't mind supporting drug dealers."

"Whatev," I protest. "Have you ever seen the delivery guys who work for Dad? Hello. They're all about the ganja. Does that make Dad a supporter of drug dealers?"

My mom throws her hands over Sweet Pea's innocent ears. "You are out of line!"

I'm out of line? She's out of line. This whole damn shopping trip is out of line! Brooke wouldn't even be pulling this stunt if Pash was here. She'd be too busy showing off, playing the perfect parent.

"C'mon, Mom, please. Just let it go," I beg.

"You know what, if you can convince your dad to let you get these shoes, then they're yours," she declares, whipping out her rhinestone cell and dialing away. I can feel the whole store watching our little drama, rooting for me. I want to tell them to keep their expectations low.

Brooke gets Earl on the phone and completely blindsides him with her propagandistic spin. Classic Brooke.

"Hi, sugar, it's me. Would you mind telling your sixteen-year-old daughter why it is inappropriate for Christians such as ourselves to buy one-hundred-and-seventy-five-dollar shoes from people who support drug dealers?" Brooke asks in her tone that tells my father "you're either with Brooke or against Brooke." And Earl never wants to be against Brooke. Ever. She hands me the phone and smugly mouths "good luck."

"Dad, it is so not even like that—"

"Girl, what do you need with a-hundred-and-seventy-five-dollar shoes?" he interrupts.

"I'm helping pay, and that is so not the point!" I counter.

"Is to me." He sighs. "Look, I don't have time to play referee. I gotta Mexican family in the middle of purchasing a full living room suite. You know those people pay cash. I gotta close this deal, so whatever your mom decides is fine by me." He hangs up.

And just like that, this day has officially become a major suck-a-thon.

On the drive home, I refuse to sit up front with my oppressor. I hang in the backseat, furiously plotting all the ways I could commit suicide and really break her heart. I imagine my funeral: the music, the casket, the flowers (all white calla lilies). And then it occurs to me that if I die my mother will get her ultimate wish. She'll get to dress me. And that thought just pisses me off even more. I vow to stay alive in protest.

I look down and discover that I'm still holding one of many band flyers I grabbed before leaving Atomic City, advertisements for concerts I'll never get to attend. At least I can use them to decorate my room.

A lime-green flyer catches my eye—a fab picture of a tough girl in '70s-style roller skates, fishnet tights, and a shredded miniskirt (a fashion statement I fully support). The ad is not for a band, but for a Roller Derby league. It reads:

Skirts, Skates, & Scrapes!
ALL THE OLD-SCHOOL SKILLS
WITH A NEW PUNK-ROCK ATTITUDE

Come See
THE LONE STAR DERBY GIRLS
AUSTIN'S ALL-GIRL ROLLER DERBY LEAGUE

THE HOLY ROLLERS VS. THE FIGHT CREW
HALFTIME CONCERT BY THE CHIMNEY SWEEPS

This ain't no cheerleading clinic, y'all!

Okay, I'm not exactly sure what this whole Roller Derby thing even is, but some inner alarm goes off inside me, and I know I have to check it out.

I glance at my mom in the front seat, blithely singing along to her bad CD as she drives closer and closer to Bodeen, taking me farther and farther from my soulmate city.

And I think, *Fuck you and your Céline Dion Muzak. The sun is quickly setting on the days when I need your permission to leave Bodeen. From now on, I'll go to Austin if I feel like it. Just try and stop me!*

 ## Hell on Wheels

*M*ajor development on the transportation front—Pash's
parents gave her a car on the first day of school (proof
they're a thousand times cooler than Brooke & Earl).

Thanks to the Pashmobile, I can now retire from
school bus–riding hell. Yes, to all you freshmen in the
back row who think armpit farts are the height of hilar-
ity, to the quartet of Corbi wannabes applying gobs of
cheap, stinky perfume, to the hicks who serenade me
each morning with your country-music-inspired gangsta
rap (a crime against humanity, trust me), and, yes, even
to Mortimor—you bus-driving fool, you, with your mis-
matched polyester socks and government-issued hearing aids—I bid you all adieu. (Thank God. I thought this
day would never come.)

Seriously, I had the single freakiest bus route in the history of freaky bus routes. And not freaky good, just freaky freaky. I know technically we are "all God's children," but one look at the people on my bus and you couldn't help but conclude God has some seriously f'ed-up offspring. And yes, I'm including myself.

But that's all behind me now. Today is the first day of the rest of my bus-free life. I hear Pash's car screech to a stop outside my window at exactly 8:32 A.M. She has the music cranked so loud the use of a horn is unnecessary. Not that it stops her. On Pash's horn-blaring cue, I slip out of my bedroom and tiptoe to our not-so-great room.

I stealthily grab my pack, throw Sweet Pea a kiss, and bolt for the door. But just as my hand reaches the knob, I hear my arch nemesis holler from the kitchen.

"Bliiiiiss! What about your breakfast?" I turn and there's Brooke in the throes of some kind of TV mom fantasy moment. She's holding a plate of piping-hot eggs, bacon, sausage, hash browns, and toast.

It's almost touching, except for the fact that I haven't eaten eggs since I was, like, five, and my vegetarianism has been in full effect for at least two years. Brooke knows this. (I sent her a press release, not to mention the monthly reminders in my "Guide to Parenting Bliss" newsletter.) She refuses to learn.

So, here she is, decked out in pearls, foisting a plate of dead animal soul in my face first thing in the morning.

Yum yum. I am *this* close to vomiting all over her Martha Stewart apron from the smell alone (& half-tempted, believe me).

But she's got this crazy look on her face, like the roof will cave in if I decline to dine, and suddenly I feel a brief but potent mix of guilt and sadness for her. I forgo my typical eye-rolling, you-don't-respect-my-beliefs monologue and do what any teen does when she is trying to get out of the house quickly in the face of a parental ambush: I kiss ass.

"Oh, my God, you're, like, the best mom ever!" I gush. "That smells amazing."

"Really? You really think so?" she asks, not wanting the real answer.

"Of course. But, Mom, do you think I could get this to go? I want to get to school in time to talk to Mrs. Luntz about trying out for cheerleader, since they're replacing Jerri Lynn Templeton," I say.

"They're replacing Jerri Lynn Templeton?" Brooke gasps with way too much excitement. "Oh, I prayed for this!"

It takes my rah-rah worshipping mother exactly twenty seconds to whip up a breakfast sandwich, wrap it in a charming little diaper-napkin, and shove it in my hand as she ushers me out the door.

"Don't be late, Bliss. Go, go, go! You're gonna be a cheerleader!"

"Thanks, Mom!" I say, kissing her cheek. I book it to Pash's car before Brooke can inhale the perfume of irony I leave behind.

Pash greets me by cranking up an appropriate classic by our beloved Ramones. (RIP, Joey!)

> Well, I don't care about history.
> Rock, rock, rock-'n'-roll high school!
> 'Cause that's not where I wanna be.
> Rock, rock, rock-'n'-roll high school . . .

I feel better already. Pash hits the gas as we zoom past my former bus stop brethren. Ciao, suckas!

Closer to school, I make Pash pull over so I can pawn my breakfast sandwich off on some all-too-eager freshman boy who looks like he hasn't had a decent meal since third grade.

"That's so Girl Scout of you," Pash remarks, applying her signature black eyeliner in the rearview.

"Not really. I'm planning on getting into a lot of trouble, so I'm trying to bank some Karma points."

"Ooh. What kind of trouble?" She smiles.

"A-hem." I clear my throat with dramatic innuendo.

"Oh riiiight, that Roller Derby thing," she taunts. "Is that this weekend? I can't remember—you've only reminded me twenty million times!"

It's true, I've nagged like a maniac 24/7, hiding reminder Post-it notes all over her room, even in her box of tampons, which she acted vaguely annoyed about (but I know she secretly loved for the creative effort).

"Oh, c'mon!" I scream. "Just say yes, already! Consider it my birthday present."

"Your birthday is six months away, dork. If I give you a gift now, you'll totally forget and then accuse me of being a crappy friend."

"Not even. If you see that my sad self gets to this Roller Derby thing, I will never accuse you of being anything more than the most awesomest best friend on the planet. Which is sayin' a lot because I'm pretty damn good myself. Oh, and did I mention, the hot-guy factor is expected to be high?"

"Damn you, Bliss, playing the hot-guy card."

"I'm just sayin'. . . ."

"Honestly," she sighs. "At this point, I'm not even sure I would recognize a genuine hottie. Do you realize the last erotic dream I had was about Ryan Seacrest—"

"Ew! That is so wrong." I gag.

"Oh, yeah," Pash says. "I went to sleep envisioning some wonderful scenario with my boyfriend, Connor Oberst, but somehow it got all jumbled, and by the time I woke up, I was muggin' down with Ryan Seacrest."

"TMI!" I scream, throwing my hands over my ears.

"Sorry, I just—"

"I am so disturbed right now," I say in full-on cringe mode.

"Clearly, my judgment is off." Pash sighs.

"Way. Which is exactly why you need to be around real boys so you can set your boy compass straight."

"You're just using me for my car," Pash says with mock suspicion.

"Your car, your clothes, your CDs—whatever you got. C'mon, Pash, my only other option is to post some skanky photos online to lure some fresh-from-prison freak out here to drive me."

"Ew! No, I will not let you skank out like that!"

"So, that means you're driving?" I say, grinning.

"Thinkin' about it. But you have to come up with a plan."

"Already workin' on it."

Rock, rock, rock, rock, rock-'n'-roll high school!

Same-O Lame-O

*E*ven though I should know better, I confess there's always a little piece of me that gets excited about the first day of school. Back in the elementary years, it was about christening a box of virgin crayons or breaking in a brand-new Sesame Street lunchbox. But these days it's more about anticipating the arrival of a perfect boyfriend in the form of an exotic exchange student or even just a really hot teacher who gets exiled to the sticks (bad for him, good for me).

By third period, it's painfully clear the foreign exchange miracle has once again eluded my grasp. Yes, friends, this year is just as lame as the last, and shocking as it sounds, my peers have somehow managed to get even more annoying over the summer.

Exhibit A: Lisa Catchum, my downstairs locker

neighbor. Now, personally, I have nothing against Lisa. That is, until her fashion choices start interfering with my pursuit of happiness, which they are in a major way. You see, Lisa is a die-hard devotee of Britney-cut jeans, and every time she bends over to get her books, I am assaulted with a major thong-a-palooza (made of gold glitter, no less—which just proves the display of ass flesh *está no accidente*).

As the day wears on, I find myself muscled out of locker access by desperate boys who jam the hallway in hopes of sneaking a peak. And Lisa doesn't disappoint. Every hour on the hour, the gold butt-floss comes out to say hello. *(Good-bye!!!!)*

"What is this, Groundhog Day?" Pash asks. "The bell can't ring unless Lisa's shown us her thong?"

"Apparently," I say, shoving past the horny onlookers.

The hourly assault on our visual senses is so disgusting that Pash and I have no choice but to spend our lunch hour drafting an anonymous letter addressing the Lisa Catchum ass-flashing issue.

Dear Lisa:
    It has come to our attention that every time you use your locker, your backside is on complete display. Perhaps you're unaware of this, perhaps you think that the breeze you

feel from bending over is the rush of the crowd passing by, or perhaps you are training to be a porn star.

Whatever your reason, it is most definitely wrong. Being forced to look at your pint-sized underwear is a distraction, and not a good one. Just because you want to flash your thong to the world doesn't mean the world wants to see it.

So, please, Lisa, for the sake of all humanity, kindly shove your ass and your Band-Aid-size panties back into your too-tight jeans, and we won't be forced to vomit on you.

Sincerely,
People for Ethical Treatment of Thongs

Bitchy? Perhaps, but desperate times call for desperate measures. Besides, you should have seen the first two drafts Pash and I whipped up, laughing till we cried into our already soggy lunchroom fries.

And when, by fifth period, Lisa takes to wearing her rhinestone hoodie around her waist for extra butt coverage, victory is mine. I can now proceed to my locker in peace.

Cowboy Yoda

*N*ow, between you, me, and Pash, there is one bright spot in this farce they call the Bodeen educational system.

That would be junior economics teacher Mr. Smiley. What can I say about this jewel of a man? He looks *exactly* like Yoda, stands maybe five foot two inches tall in his high-heeled cowboy boots, and is a die-hard devotee of Western suits. And when I say Western suits, I don't mean any ol' just-add-water cowboy getup. I mean the polyester kind they quit making sometime in the '70s, the kind that only came in pastel colors usually reserved for special-issue M&M's at Easter. Peach, lemon, lavender, mint green—Mr. Smiley has the entire collection, and then some. He must have stockpiled them as their expiration date was coming up.

Normally, such a bold fashion move from a teacher in the face of judgmental teens would result in abject ridicule (witness Mrs. Gomer and her wacky "Friday earrings"). But Mr. Smiley deftly avoids such pitfalls.

He never lets anyone forget that, despite being 108 years old and a charter member of the pastel appreciation society, he could kick your teenage ass in a heartbeat. Not even the toughest boys dare fuck with Mr. S.

And if the fashion glory weren't enough to convince you of his greatness, consider his legendary use of nicknames. Mr. Smiley has a moniker for every student who crosses his path—Slick, Hee-haw, Black Jack, Ladybug, Rawhide, Pop Tart. . . .

He'll swagger through the halls, urging kids to get to class. "Skedaddle, Lipstick. Bell's about to ring," he'll say in his exaggerated Texas drawl. "You too, Cracker Jack. And take Hopscotch and Johnny Diamond with ya. . . . Wanda Sue, I'm lookin' at you. . . . Time's up, Lion Tamer. . . . Dorito, you are not exempt. . . ."

In my brief run-ins with Mr. Smiley, I have been referred to as Betty Rebel, Firecracker, Outlaw, Bohemian Rhapsody, and Ginger Snap.

He never uses the same nickname twice. Ever. Sometimes I think that when Mr. Smiley finally does pass on to that big classroom in the sky, it won't be because of a heart attack or anything like that. It will be because he finally ran out of nicknames.

He owns his weirdness in such a pure way, just thinking about it makes me want to cry. I totally worship him, which is why I dedicate my back-to-school fashion statement to him—a homemade T-shirt that says MR. SMILEY IS MY HOMEBOY in iron-on velvet letters.

When I take a seat in seventh period, Cowboy Yoda regards the garment with guarded suspicion, but I flash him my sincere smile to let him know I'm legit (the smile I save for Pash and the boyfriend I have yet to meet). Mr. Smiley warms. His pointy ears even twitch with approval.

"Well, Blueberry," he declares, "it's high time I had me a fan club."

"No doubt," I say. And we exchange a high five, which my clueless classmates regard with slack-jawed confusion, trying to decide whether or not it's cool. (Clearly it is.)

They Skate by Night

*F*riday night, 8:23 P.M. Pash and I are driving approximately 102 miles an hour to get to Austin in time for our Roller Derby baptism.

We scam Pash's parents with a heartwarming tale about two girls who love rooting for their high school football team so much they can't bear to miss the season opener against Killean High, two hours away. Since being a "normal American teenager" trumps all in the immigrant Amini household, they agree to extend Pash's car curfew to one A.M. which gives us just enough time to dip our toes in the water of real fun. Naturally, I'm also spending the night, which keeps our plan safely under the Brooke radar. Woo hoo!

I'm so amped in the car, I change my clothes a

thousand times in search of fashion greatness. With the pickin's slim, I settle into my old standby, a micro minidress made from a vintage T-shirt and held together with nothing but a million strategically placed safety pins. I wear it layered over tights to undercut the would-be slut factor. Normally I love wearing this dress, but tonight I'm just not feeling it. I'm afraid my romance with my favorite frock might be over.

"I'm so sick of all my clothes," I say, fishing in the backseat for options I haven't yet explored. Pash slaps my hand and shouts over the "Tunes for a Roller Derby Road Trip" mix I made especially for the momentous occasion.

"No more changes!" she yells. "You look smokin' in that dress, so stop bein' such an insecure girlie-girl. You're about to make me wreck the Pashmobile."

"Don't you think the dress has too many safety pins?" I ask.

"There's no such thing as too many safety pins! Besides," she adds, completely contradicting the confidence she just displayed, "*I'm* the one with a fashion fatality here."

Pash lifts her freshly dyed, bright-red hair to reveal the Manic Panic residue that makes an impromptu necklace along the back of her neck.

"I warned you about solo dying," I say. "Not for beginners."

"I know, but I was crazy bored and needed a break

from studying my French. It was either that or I was gonna eat half a chocolate cake. I chose to dye my hair."

"See, that's what you get from too much studying," I say, "bad beauty judgment and no dessert."

Pash shrugs and frowns at the road.

"Actually, your hair looks fab," I say. "Just wear it down, and nobody will notice the spillage."

"You think?"

"I think."

"What about when I'm makin' out with a guy and—"

"Makin' out with a guy? My, my, someone has big plans for tonight."

"Always."

"Well, if he asks, just tell him it's a tattoo. Of a giant red amoeba."

She laughs and turns up the music. That's my Pash.

Our People

We finally make it to Austin but get so tragically lost trying to locate the elusive warehouse district (thanks for *nothing*, Internet directions!), we nearly miss the whole freakin' thing. Literally, we're like the last two people they let in before tickets sell out.

But one step inside and I know my little nag-a-thon has paid off. Big time. In Bodeen, a "hot Friday night" consists of a bunch of hick teenagers circling the Sonic Drive-In with their parent-issued pickup trucks. But this, this is the real thing—high school alternateens seamlessly mingling with cool college folks. You have to understand that in my deprived-of-interesting-people state, just being around several hundred cool people is more than a little overwhelming. It's a goddamn miracle.

Am I even allowed to be in a place this cool? Surely something will disrupt it. The World Order for Fun will put an emergency call in to Brooke and she'll show up and cart me away. *That was a close one—you almost had fun, there. Back to the sticks with you.*

Pash, thankfully, is not given to such paranoid brain spasms. She tilts her head back, opens her arms, and declares happily, "These . . . are our people."

"Totally," I say before laying eyes on a troll-lookin' dude gracelessly chugging a can of Lone Star beer. "Except for him. He is not our people."

"Ew, yeah, not him—everyone but him."

Troll aside, the derby fan base offers up lustworthy lads as far as the eye can see (and the eye can see pretty darn far).

So, while we're waiting for the Derby Girls to do their skating thing, Pash and I engage in some primo cute boy crowd scanning (CBCS).

"Okay," Pash whispers, "what about him, tall boy in the Buddy Holly glasses?"

"Yum. But ohmygod—check out cigarette-behind-the-ear boy over here." I motion subtly to my right.

"Ooh! Just looking at him makes me want to smoke." She sighs.

"No doubt."

"Let's go bum a cigarette from him," she declares, linking her arm in mine and dragging me in his direction.

"No!" I say, putting on the brakes.

"Okay, Ms. I'll Wear a Sexy Little Minidress but I'm Too Afraid to Talk to a Boy. You are such a wuss."

"I'm not a wuss," I protest. "I'm just . . . flirtation impaired."

"Wait! Him! Look, look—my future husband over there," Pash squeals, flicking her head wildly to the right like an epileptic. A really cute epileptic.

"Jesus, what is it with you and Mohawk boys?" I ask.

"What *isn't* it with me and Mohawk boys!" Pash declares.

And just as we're discussing this, Mohawk Boy turns toward us. Not missing a beat, Pash throws him a finely calibrated low-key smile. He answers with a sly what's-up? nod.

I feel the sudden urge to get out of the line of flirtation fire so Pash and MB can do their thing.

I turn my gaze to the floor, trying to disappear. Looking at the sea of shoes, it occurs to me that practically everyone here is wearing Converse low-tops. (*Converse here, Converse there, Converse, Converse everywhere!*) Thank God that Pash let me borrow her go-go boots tonight, because as much as I love my classic Chucks, it's abundantly clear they are on the fast track to becoming a cliché. Just like skulls. One has to get out of Bodeen to observe such dynamic shifts in indie fashion.

Among the mass of too-cool-for-school canvas sneakers, I spot a pair of scuffed-up wingtips covered in paint splatters. Could these be the shoes of an interesting artist boy? I am immediately intrigued. My eyes follow the paint-stained brogues up to a pair of weathered jeans, a threadbare T-shirt, and last but definitely not least, a shock of messy ink-black hair. If he looks this good from the back . . .

. . . And then he turns. The entire place becomes a blur as this smoldering lad comes into sharp focus. His messy hair (I'm a total sucker for bed-head) is even better from the front, half of it sliding into his emerald eyes. I repeat, *emerald eyes.* Not to mention the lanky, rocker-boy bod and pasty complexion that suggests too much time spent indoors listening to records. In short, per-fec-tion.

And even though Señor Smolder is so obviously a winner in nature's oddball beauty lottery, he looks like he spends exactly .0002 seconds thinking about it—which only makes him hotter. It is halfway through this thought that I suddenly realize SS is looking my direction—*right at me.* My stomach erupts into a mess of flip-flops and untamed butterflies. And then, everything goes black.

Okay, please tell me that I did not just pass out over some guy I have never met. Please, please, please let me take comfort in knowing that even I am not that lame.

And then I hear a wall of cheers rise up around me and I realize I'm still standing. It's the lights that went out, not me. Disaster dodged. Whew—that was close.

Pash grabs my hand as the crush of derby humanity carries us to the track where the derby madness is about to begin. I look back, but Señor Smolder has vanished in the dark.

Roller Derby Baptism

*T*he anticipation of the derby-hungry crowd builds to such a fevered pitch, I begin to think the roof of the warehouse might just blow off and fly away. But then—*fwoom!*—spotlights rain down on the track and the show comes hurtling at us at a hundred miles an hour. As good as the guy watching is, these girls quickly serve up their own brand of irresistible entertainment.

First, the Fight Crew skates out onto the track. They're a team of surly flight attendants, decked out in killer kitschy '60s-style stewardess dresses (I have mod fashion envy from their uniforms alone). Not to mention, they all have amazing names like Holly Go-Fightly, Eva Destruction, and Kami Kazzi. A couple of them throw drinks and bags of peanuts from a beverage cart into the crowd.

Then come the Holy Rollers, a busload of bad-ass Catholic schoolgirls. Their uniforms consist of—you guessed it—plaid miniskirts, set off by torn fishnet tights and lots of tattoos (more fashion envy). They too have cool monikers like Annie Social, Helena Handbasket, and Dinah Might, the girl from the poster.

But the team intros are just an appetizer for the four-course meal that follows—the skating.

Honestly, I'm still not even sure what the rules of Roller Derby are, but from the first whistle to the last the night becomes a blur of high-speed skating and breath-taking stunts. It's hands-down the most awe-inspiring thing I've ever seen in my entire life. Girls dive on the track, leap over one another, pile on the infield for brawls, fly over the rails into the crowd (more than once!), and basically tear one another apart . . . and yet, you can tell they are having the time of their lives. It's '70s B-movie heaven.

And Dinah Might of the Holy Rollers—oh, my God! She's tiny, with fragile features, but her skating is "pure TNT," as they say. I love her the way boys love Superman. I want to be her.

When it's all said and done, the Holy Rollers beat the Fight Attendants with a score of 72 to 44, but that is *so* beside the point!

If punk rock were a sport run by surly chicks on roller skates, the result would be Roller Derby. Every one of the Derby Girls is completely gorgeous in her own way: There are skinny girls, chubby girls, tall girls, short girls, girls with big butts, girls with big boobs, girls with no boobs, girls with tattoos, girls without—and the crowd adores them all. In short, it's the most Bliss-friendly activity I've ever seen, so refreshingly antipageant. I'm a total convert.

When the derby action wraps up, the warehouse becomes a giant party with the Derby Girls mingling with the crowd. But before I can actually meet one of my new heroes, Pash waves her Hello Kitty Timex in my face.

"It's 12:07," she says. "We gotta book."

"But I'm not done having fun."

"If I don't have time to hook up with a hot guy, you don't have time to play Roller Derby groupie," she barks, prodding me to the exit like best-friend cattle. The girl does not mess around with the curfew gods.

And just as we're leaving, we pass the merch table, where the Derby Girls sell everything from T-shirts to trading cards. They have their own trading cards! As if pulled by derby gravity, I break away from Pash to get a closer look.

I find myself face-to-face with a fierce platinum blonde sporting blue streaks that I hate to admit look better on her than they ever did on me. Not to mention the killer mermaid tattoo covering her left arm. She furrows her cool brow and gives me a look that suggests she's deciding whether or not to kick my ass.

Before I can censor myself, the following falls out of my mouth: "Y'all are my new heroes! I wanna be you!" I gush, like some thirteen-year-old at her first boy band concert at Six Flags.

"Then get your ass on the track and make it happen," she says, with friendly encouragement. "As much fun as Roller Derby is to watch, it's even more fun to play."

"Oh, I could never," I say. "I mean, I haven't even touched my Barbie roller skates since, like, fifth grade."

"Whatever," she says. "It all comes back. We're having tryouts on Tuesday. You should check it out."

Come to think of it, my elementary school years included a pretty intense roller-skating phase. Bikes and Razor scooters may have been the method of transport for my peers, but skates were my thing. And just like that—an idea that five minutes ago would have seemed utterly insane now seems completely logical.

"I'm so in!" I suddenly snort, taking my dorkiness to new heights. For the record, I have never snorted in my life, but here I am expressing myself through pig noises. So lame.

"You just have to be eighteen—you're eighteen, right?" I feel Pash walk up and give me the silent stare of death, which I ignore.

"Uh, yeah, I just had my birthday," I lie.

"Cool. I'm Malice," she says, "Malice in Wonderland."

"Awesome. I'm Bliss—" She gives me a look that says,

You have got to be kidding me with that name. "But I can totally change that."

"You'll need to," Malice says, with a cool smile.

"We're going now," Pash suddenly says, kiboshing the convo and dragging me out by the sleeve.

On the way to the Pashmobile, I can barely contain myself, skipping all the way. Pash turns sharply to me.

"Okay, what the hell was that?" she asks.

"What the hell was what?"

"You can't play Roller Derby!" she practically shouts.

"Let's try out together," I say, in between skips. "It will be so fun!"

"Um, excuse me, getting pummeled by a bunch of badass chicks on skates is not my idea of fun. For the record, I didn't have a Barbie roller-skating phase, okay? I had a 'fat kid sits inside and reads a book' phase. Unlike *some* people," she adds, "I know my limits."

"What's that supposed to mean?"

"Those girls are seriously tough. And, Bliss, you"—she grabs my unsuspecting arm and twists it into an Indian sunburn so brutal I yelp out loud—"are not tough."

"Well, not yet," I say meekly. "But maybe I could be."

"Whatever. Your mom's gonna fuh-reak."

"No she won't. She'll never know," I say. As if I would ever tell Brooke I'm taking up Roller Derby.

"Ooh," Pash says with sudden approval, "you are one risk-taking bitch."

"C'mon," I prod. "Just try it with me."

"I'm not sacrificing my GPA," Pash says firmly, unlocking the car.

Once again I am reminded that my best friend is a pre-premed genius, and all those As that dutifully line up on her report card are no accident. She's the academic rock star; I'm the academic roadie.

"It won't be nearly as fun without my Pash," I say sadly, ending several seconds of silence.

"If you make it," she says, "I'll come to every game to cheer your fine ass on." I feel better already.

We race back to Bodeen to beat the parental clock. Pash swings by Sonic so we can get the football score from the lame but useful late-night tailgaters. It is 1:02 (well within the five-minute grace period) when we stroll through the door singing a school fight song we made up in the car.

"How was the game?" asks Mr. Amini.

"Amazing," Pash answers. "We won."

"Fourteen to three," I add, providing the legitimate detail to our fiction.

When we get to her room, Pash and I can't shut the door fast enough before erupting with conspiratorial laughter and flopping on her perpetually unmade bed.

Bingo

*T*he next morning I colonize Pash's computer to do a little online derby research, an activity I don't dare try at home for two reasons. One, the homestead of Earl and Brooke is not exactly a hotbed of modern technology. They are painfully stuck in the dark ages of Internet dial-up (literally, you can watch a zit come and go on your face while that sad PC wheezes its way to a Web connection). And two, on the rare occasion you possess the saintlike patience to use the slow-mo computer, there is a 103 percent chance that Brooke will be hovering nearby, eagle-eyeing your every click.

I'd rather not subject myself to such surveillance, thankyouverymuch.

So, while Pash snores her Saturday away, I help myself to a couple (okay, four) of the Pop-Tarts she keeps stashed behind her stereo and settle in to some quality time with the Derby Girls Web site. I learn that the girls are having tryouts for their upcoming season on Tuesday at seven P.M.

Tryouts—there's a terrifying word for ya. Sure, it sounds so innocent and casual, but I've never actually tried out for anything in my life. The idea alone makes me so nervous I'm already sweating more than my aunt Brenda at a Fourth of July picnic, and believe me, that woman can sweat.

And yet. Something about watching those Derby Girls and hearing their skates pound on the track—it's like I got to peek through the window at what life could be like outside of Bodeen. I want more. I need more. Nerves be damned, I have to get back to that window. I want to open it and climb through.

If I could just line up a little transpo. The Pashmobile is no go, but there is this matter of the Bodeen Bingo Bus for Senior Citizens, a chariot that shuttles local old folks to the Bingo Palace in Austin every Tuesday and Thursday so they can get their B-7 and N-65 on. (Note: Bodeen sucks so hard that even our senior citizens have to leave to have a good time.)

Perhaps they won't mind a stowaway.

The Geritol Jitney

*E*ventually I may have to go into my little lab of lies and whip up a long-term alibi to cover my Roller Derby escapades, but for now I tell Brooke I'm at Pash's working on my *Scarlet Letter* paper.

I dig my abandoned Barbie skates from beneath a graveyard of stuffed animals in the back of my closet, blow off the dust, and wrestle my overgrown foot into one. They don't exactly fit, but at least I can get them laced. I stuff them in my book bag and lug them around all day at school. The final bell cannot ring fast enough.

When Pash drops me off at the Bodeen Senior Center, a dozen golden oldies have boarded the bus, and they're already pulling away.

I have to chase it down, waving my arms—"Wait!

Wait!" The driver, a hillbilly burnout named Todd, who favors the no-shirt look to set off a thinning ponytail that has clearly seen better days, pulls over and pops the door.

I say "thanks," hop aboard, and find myself suddenly squaring off against a gang of ornery old folks. These people are very territorial about their bingo shuttle. They're not about to give up an empty seat to a sixteen-year-old. For a moment, I half expect them to chase me off with their canes and walkers. Note to self: Do not come between a senior citizen and his bingo schedule.

It takes some on-the-fly wheeling and dealing—and a teeny tiny lie about being on my way to visit "my sick grandma" in Austin—before Helen, a sweet old thing rockin' a pair of red Keds, steps up on my behalf.

"She's with me. And if y'all don't like it, you can go suck an egg," Helen declares, patting the seat next to her.

"Thanks," I say, taking her up on her offer. I notice her tightly curled helmet of hair is dyed old-lady blue. "I love your hair color."

"Thanks. I do it m'self," she says, handing me a ball of yarn to hold as she knits.

I tune out the rest of my scowling bingo-bound buds with my iPod (that great savior of awkward social situations). An hour later, the van pulls in front of the Bingo Palace, and I hop a bus downtown that drops me off two blocks from the warehouse. I book it down a back alley and make it just in time.

Initiation Nation

As soon as I get to the warehouse, aka the Dollhouse, the place falls into an intimidating hush. Forty girls all turn at once and look curiously at me like I'm an invader—at least it feels that way. I'm so used to not giving a crap about what anyone thinks of me, but I'm suddenly hit by a tidal wave of insecurity.

On the cool scale, these girls are a ten. On a good day I'm a two-point-seven. I feel like the sad mathlete awkwardly trying to infiltrate the cheerleader clique at lunch in every bad teen movie you wish you'd never seen (except you have, several times). And we all know these scenarios do not end well. Especially for the mathlete.

Look at them with their casual badassness, decked out in shredded band T-shirts and cut-off Dickies, already comparing derby names.

"I'm gonna be Princess Slaya," one fierce-looking tall girl says. I haven't even begun to think of a derby name.

I admit it, I want them to like me. Fuck that, I want them to love me. Damn Pash and her Harvard ambitions, leaving me to venture into the cruel world alone.

What if they ID me and find out I'm only sixteen? I should take my loser ass and run while I can. If I hurry, I can still make the bingo game with Helen.

But a voice shakes me out of my self-loathing daydream. "You made it." I turn to see Malice heading over with her skates coolly draped over her shoulder. I smile and give a dorky wave.

Malice kindly overlooks my lack of social skills and takes me inside. She hooks me up with elbow pads, wrist guards, knee pads, and a helmet.

When I finally get all geared up, I bravely climb onto the track and—*BAM!*—immediately fall on my newbie ass. The humiliation can barely register before two girls are there to help me up. "Don't worry about it," they say. "You're just starting."

Yeah. Easy for them to say as they practice jumping over orange traffic cones set up on the track. I stumble around like newborn Bambi learning to walk. Only I fall more than Bambi ever did. The earth revolves around the sun four times before I make it around the track just once. And then a whistle blows marking the end of our warm-up. Let me recap: I skate / fall my way around the track just once, and the warm-up is already over!

All fifteen girls trying out line up on the infield of the track. At a quick glance, I can tell every one of these girls could kick my ass.

Then the six team captains introduce themselves. There's Juana Beat'n of the Sirens, the bad cops. She's curvy hot in that J.Lo sex-bomb way—if J.Lo were cool and not the cheesy she-robot that she is. Next is Eva Destruction, a pale Goth, who is head of the Fight Crew. Tinker Hell, a girlie blonde who looks like she'd be more at home on the tennis court, runs the Black Widows, while Joan Threat, a spiky-haired indie rock girl, heads up the Cherry Bombs. Malice is captain of the Hurl Scouts. And last, but certainly not least, is Dinah Might of the "undefeated Holy Rollers."

I'm so starstruck when Dinah introduces herself, I blurt out, "You're the reason I'm here!" The room falls to a hush, all heads turn to me, and Dinah says, "Um, yeah, kissing my ass is not going to get you on my team." Okay, I've just offended the coolest girl in the room. Off to a smashing start.

We launch into a series of drills to show our raw skills. The idea is that the teams can teach us Roller Derby. We just have to show them we can skate. Between you and me, I was always an awesome skater as a kid—I lived on those wheels—but there is little lingering evidence of it this evening.

The whole thing is such a blur of humiliation. Here are the highlights: (a) I spend more time on my ass than on my skates. (b) At one point, I feel Dinah looking at my pink Barbie skates. Her look of disapproval makes me fall. (c) When we all have to skate around in a "pack," bumping each other to show we're not afraid to take or give a hit, I hover a good six feet behind, too afraid to engage.

We take a water break, and I can feel the collective pity vibe. I'm the girl other girls feel sorry for. It's a good thing I'm sweating so much—it hides the tears I can feel coming on.

A whistle blows, signaling the end of the water break. We line up for time trials. All we have to do is skate around the track five times as fast as we can. As we get back on the track, Malice grabs my arm.

"Hey," she says, "quit judging yourself. Just try to have fun, okay?"

"Okay," I say, touched, but not knowing what the hell I'm going to do with that advice.

One by one, derby hopefuls run through their time trials. A couple of girls fall but get back up and keep going; others ease their way around the track. Most show some basic understanding of "skating the track," but no one's breaking any speed records, that's for damn sure. *All I have to do is get around the track five times. I can do this.*

I line up, the whistle blows, and I immediately stumble as I take off. I keep skating, fighting my wobbles, and get around the track one time with relative ease (yes!). But then something clicks on the second lap. I lean low into the track, push as hard as I can, and—bingo—I go flying out of the turn at speeds the other girls haven't even touched. For a second, it feels like I might not be able to control the speed, but I bend my knees lower and manage to go even faster. From there on, the track is mine. I attack it with all I have.

When I finish my fifth lap, Tinker Hell looks up from her stopwatch and shouts, "Twenty-two-point-four seconds!" (Half the time the other girls clocked.)

Not knowing how to stop, I slam into the rail and fall on the track. Everyone applauds, and I lie there, panting, feeling proud but a little stunned. I didn't know I had that in me. I suddenly wonder what else I have in me that's been stunted by too many years of pageant participation.

I have to sprint back to the bus stop to make it to the bingo shuttle in time, which I do. Barely.

The seniors are whining about the "fixed game" they just experienced, while Helen counts her winnings in the corner. That crafty minx.

Me and Helen, we're both winners tonight.

Tough Cookie

*S*o, the next day at school I limp up to Pash, and she gives me this tragic look.

"What happened to you? You look like you got your ass kicked."

"Oh, I totally did." I smile. "But guess what. I made it! I'm a Hurl Scout!" Yep, Malice, who I have officially adopted as my derby fairy godmother, drafted me for her team.

"Congratulations!" Pash says. "I'm so proud of you!"

"I know," I say. "Now, all I have to do is get a real pair of skates, change my work schedule, and—" Pash goes white and gives me the patented serious-best-friend face.

"What? No! The only reason that godforsaken job doesn't drive me to a murderous rampage is because we have the same schedule. You *can't* change it, Bliss." Now, as much as I heart and adore Pash, there's no way I'm not doing Roller Derby. Life outside of Bodeen starts with derby.

"We'll always have Fridays," I say, putting my arm around her.

"I hate you," she says, putting her arm around me.

After much consideration and rehearsal in front of my bedroom mirror, I explain to the 'rents that my new Tuesday / Thursday absence from home is because I have joined a study group to prep for my SATs.

Brooke looks up from pinning a costume on Sweet Pea. "You know, Bliss, that's not a bad idea," she says, her tiara-hunting wheels spinning. "Smart girls are all the rage in pageants these days, and you can bet your biscuit the Miss Bluebonnet judges will be impressed by that."

Do you see what I have to deal with here? My own mother doesn't want me to be smart for the sake of being smart, or for the sake of, oh, I dunno, *going to college—* she wants me smart for a beauty pageant. Could someone (anyone) please tell her this is the twenty-first century?

The Anti–High School

I'm early for my first official Hurl Scouts practice.
I already have my gear on when the other girls start fil-
ing in the door.

Once the casual warm-up is done, Coach Brian, aka
Blade, puts us to work. A word about Blade. He's maybe
twenty-three years old, sort of cute in a tacky, metalhead
geek, gold-chain-wearing kind of way (which means in
any other circumstance, we would have nothing to say
to each other). But it just so happens that Blade loves
roller skating and is amazing at it, which makes him a
dork to most of society but a god to us.

Even when Blade is kicking our asses with skating
drills, the girls are on a nonstop quest to get him to blush
with their raunchy jokes, which keeps things so fun you

almost (almost) forget how hard you're sweating. It's the kind of hilarious vibe that you would never see in the coach-as-screaming-dictator world of high school sports. Roller Derby is so anti-that.

Most of my teammates are college students (a few are even over twenty-one—hint, hint). No one questions my underage status, though I do tell them a little fib about living in Bodeen, working at the Oink Joint to save for college, which they assume means I've already graduated (and I, for one, have no intention of correcting them).

Life is already getting better. I'm like the adopted little sister they are all looking out for, which I love.

And for the record, the Roller Derby sisterhood is the real thing, not tainted by that fake you-go-girl, Oprah vibe you get from Noxzema commercials (which I'm deeply allergic to). And this is how I really know. No one actually says "you go, girl." It's more like "you kick ass" or "you rock the house with that shit," but not that stupid "you go, girl" crap.

My assignment for next practice, other than mastering the skills of skating, is to come up with a derby name, as everyone agrees Bliss is not gonna cut it. (I've been telling Brooke that for years.)

Metamorphosis

The next three weeks fly by as my life becomes all derby, all the time. I order my own pair of skates using my would-be John Fluevog shoe money. Naturally I have them shipped to Pash's house so as not to arouse suspicion from Brooke. We tell her parents the box is a telescope, and they approve.

At practice, the humiliation factor decreases as my skating improves. Even though I'm covered in bruises, aka "derby kisses," I feel surprisingly proud of what I'm learning to do. (It's so weird; I'm kind of like a jock.) I even sneak out late at night to covertly practice my T-stops and power slides in the driveway, determined to catch up to the other girls.

I love the way the wind whips through my hair at

practice as I fly through the turns, sitting low, leaning into the track for maximum speed. My life feels like it has been so slow for so long, it's fun to finally be going fast.

Now if I could just master the blocking thing. You know, the part of the sport that makes it Roller *Derby* and not just roller *skating*. So far, every time Emma Geddon or Crystal Deth or Malice lean into me for a little contact, I immediately fall to the ground.

After one of these signature episodes, Blade skates up to me and says, "It's a contact sport, Bliss. That means that eventually *you will have to make contact*."

Okay, he has a point. But I still feel like shit for being called on it.

Meanwhile, I bug Pash day in, day out, constantly consulting her (she would say harassing) about the perfect Roller Derby name. We can be having a perfectly random convo about why Principal Starsiak is a total hag and then I'll say "What about Punky Bruiser? Or Maggie Mayhem? Or Raggedy Annarchy?"

When I try to bring it up again, Pash finally just rolls her eyes. "If you start the name thing, I'm not coming to your game."

"That's cool," I say, "because Malice and I already have it covered."

"You actually picked a name? Spit it out," Pash says.

"Nope. You have to wait for the game," I say, leaving her in the hall as I disappear into my English class.

In the Derby Closet

The surprising thing about my double derby life is that I know I have to be in perfect-child mode to avoid Brooke. And listening to the old people bicker on the bingo bus, my survival tactic is to keep my headphones cranked high and my nose in my books. As long as I have one hand holding Helen's ball of knitting yarn, I can do no wrong.

So, in the height of rebelling and lying to my parents, I manage to bring home the kind of grades I haven't seen since second grade. Straight As. Vintage Bliss.

It's amazing—you can get away with anything as long as your report card is bragworthy. Why did I not work this strategy earlier?

Even Earl pulls me aside and sweetly places a hundred-dollar bill in my palm. "I'm real proud of ya, kiddo," he says. The whole exchange nearly makes me erupt in tears because normally Earl's not one for involvement. Plus, even though I'm over most everything these days, I'm not over my dad calling me kiddo. I hope I never am.

A Smashing Debut

*T*his is it, this is the night—my debut as the one, the only Babe Ruthless before a crowd of adoring fans. Even better, Sadie, Juana, and their roommate Octavia (who we call Rocktavia because she does) have planned an insane after-party at their house.

Finally (finally), my real life is about to begin, and I'm taking Pash with me. Actually, when I mentioned the after-party, Pash responded, "You are so dead if I'm not invited." As if she even had to ask.

I wouldn't dare go to an after-party without my Pash Amini.

We pulled the ol' "I'm spending the night at Pash's house, and she's spending the night at my house" parental switcheroo. Normally this scheme would arouse major suspicion with Brooke, but a fortuitous turn of events helped our cause. Brooke had to accompany Sweet Pea to a Little Miss Whatever pageant in Dallas, leaving me in the care of my not-so-tuned-in-to-the-rules father.

Do I feel bad finking out on Earl when lately he's been so nice? Put it this way: Bliss feels guilty, but Babe Ruthless knows the derby show must go on.

Pash and I have been handed a golden opportunity to stay out all night. We intend to take full advantage of it.

Tonight the league of Derby Girls is represented by the Sirens, a team of crooked she-cops, and the Hurl Scouts, a gang of Girl Scouts gone bad.

We can hear the crowd filling the warehouse as we get costumed up. Crystal Deth hooks me up with some fab eye makeup that would make any *Rocky Horror* devotee melt with envy. And when I finally don my adorable green Girl Scout dress with my shredded acid-green-and-black fishnet tights, I nearly cry. I look hot and scary all at once—my kind of fabulous.

When they announce Babe Ruthless, I take my lap around the track, emptying a box of Thin Mints on the crowd. It's hard to tell who is having more fun: me or them. Me, I think.

Malice picks me out to be the first jammer (point scorer) for our team. The whistle blows and something erupts in me. I take off as if I were shot out of a cannon, weaving and sidestepping the opposing blockers who try to take me down. They miss.

I even manage to take a beautiful "whip" off Emma Gedden coming into a turn. She throws her arm out behind her, I grab on, and her force slings me out of the turn, sending me ahead of all the Sirens. It's a crowd-pleasing move, that's for damn sure.

When time runs out, I have managed to rack up an impressive six points for the Hurl Scouts. (Which I know is not the point, but c'mon, it's my first time!)

My adrenaline is through the roof, and I have to sit out the jam just to catch my breath and manage a killer case of cottonmouth. I guzzle a bottle of water, scanning the crowd for boys.

Of course I'm keeping an eye out for a glimpse of Señor Smolder, the delicious rocker boy who has haunted my every waking daydream since I first laid eyes on him nearly six weeks ago. Cute boys every-where, but alas, no SS.

Just as well—he was probably a mirage. Or even worse, not actually that hot (his hotness being a figment of my imagination). If I saw him now I would probably be disappointed to the point of being creeped out. And I'm having too much fun for such romantic letdowns. I'm playing Roller Derby!

Before halftime, Crystal hurts her knee and has to sit out a few jams. During a time-out, Malice calls me to block. I give her a you-must-be-crazy look. It's well established that blocking's not my strong suit.

Malice pulls me aside and says, "You know what I do when I have to block? I think of my ex-boyfriend, Dax, and what an asshole he was—a word of advice, Ruthless, never date a boy in a band, or a Leo—they're totally toxic. Anyway, when I block, I picture kicking Dax's ass with his precious guitar. It totally helps. Think of things that piss you off, and you'll throw some great blocks."

So, I'm up there blocking, and Robin Graves is jamming, poised to pass me and score. Normally, I'd let Robin go, but not this time. This time I follow Malice's advice. I think of Brooke, and Corbi, and all the cranky customers who never tip—all of it—and just as Robin goes low to pass, I throw my hip and shoulder and—*bingo*—I make contact. Robin slams to the track as I skate away.

By the final heat, I'm so goin' with the flow, I feel invincible and, dare I say, ruthless. This time I'm blocking, not jamming. I can do whatever stunt I want. And somehow, with the crowd egging us on to a big finish, I go for the granddaddy stunt of them all: taking the rail.

Only three girls in the league can really pull this off, but somehow I decide I'm going to be the fourth. So, I take a hit from Juana Beat'n of the Sirens and head to the top of the track full speed. When I hit the edge, I reach for the rail and cartwheel myself right over.

The drop is about eight feet onto cold, hard concrete.

The crowd gasps. . . . I see nothing but a blur of lights as I fly through the air. . . .

And then—*SLAP!*—my skates hit the floor. The crowd roars, and I realize I'm still standing. I did it! I took the fucking rail!

And just like that, I'm a Derby Girls legend, in my own mind anyway. The minute I step off the track I can feel my social life taking a sharp turn for the better. I am swarmed by fans.

Pash runs over, swatting them all away, screaming, "Oh, my God, Bliss! You're a freakin' rock star!"

A charming but much-too-old dude steps up. "You rock, Babe Ruthless," he says, starting to hand me a beer.

Malice steps in like a protective lioness. "She's only eighteen, asshole," she barks, shoving the old dude away.

"But I wanted that beer," I whine.

"We'll get you one at the party," Malice says.

Make-out Island

By the time Pash and I arrive to make our grand party entrance, the surrounding streets are so packed with cars, we practically have to park in Bodeen. Not that I'm complaining. The epic walk is so worth it.

The place is amok with hotties. Margaritas and Lone Stars pass through the hands of partyers like punch at a five-year-old's birthday. And Pash wastes no time helping herself to the alcohol and the boys.

I don't know how, but I get sidelined by some icky skate-rat named Adam who's maybe fourteen years old while my fellow Derby Girls seem to have no problem poaching the more desirable picks.

By twelve-thirty, Derby HQ becomes Make-out HQ. On the lawn, in the kitchen, in the hallway, in the bedrooms, in both bathrooms, and even in the backyard, couples are hooking up. Everyone but me, and I can't seem to get rid of Icky, who follows me from room to room as I look for Pash, who has vanished.

On the verge of boredom-tears, I elect myself DJ and take over the stereo. (We've been listening to the same Beck CD for two hours, and that's just wrong—even if you do like Beck.)

I sort through Rocktavia's record collection, searching for sonic inspiration. A Velvet Underground and Nico album catches my eye. I think how I often see this band referenced in music articles but still haven't actually heard them. Sometimes I just want to explain to the music snobs that I'm only sixteen, and I've only been listening to real music for two years. *Give me some time to catch up!*

I throw the record on the turntable, curious to see for myself what the Velvet hubbub is all about. The needle hits the vinyl, the music starts, and . . . *ohmyfreakin'god.* I am beyond blown away.

They're not at all what I was expecting, a loud punk hybrid. What's coming out of the stereo is like a genre unto itself, a charming, fucked-up fairy tale that immediately breaks my heart in all the best ways.

I stretch out on the floor with my ear parked next to the speaker, in a trance. I place the album cover over my face to block out any interruption as "I'll Be Your Mirror" seduces me. I immediately add the song to my mental list of top ten songs ever.

And as I'm bobbing my head with dreamy abandon, I hear a voice. "Nice choice, DJ," it says.

I slowly slide the album cover down past my eyes and look up. My eyes spy his shoes first—*paint splattered brogues*. My heart stops when I look at his face. Pale skin, messy black hair, emerald eyes . . . Señor Smolder! He's eighteen, maybe nineteen. And no, my imagination didn't lie, he is just as devastating now as he was the first time I saw him. Only even more, because he just complimented my taste in music.

I quickly roll over and stand up. Just looking at him, I'm struck with a lightning bolt of swoon. The current rips through me, and I literally stumble forward—he has to hold out his arm to steady me.

"Head rush," I say, trying to regain my breath and my dignity.

"This album will do that to ya."

"It's incredible. I never heard it before now."

"Really?" he asks, with interest. "So what do you think?"

Now, if you are the type of person who experiences deep feelings of embarrassment mixed with cringiness when someone makes a complete fool of herself, I suggest you skip ahead. Otherwise, here are the gory details.

"Well," I say, "you know how sometimes people are all, 'Man, this the best album on the planet! You have not lived until you have heard this!'? And then you listen, and you're, like, 'Whatever, I'm so not impressed'? But, other times, you hear a band for the first time, and it's so good it just makes your stomach hurt in the best way? Um, I guess this is one of those times. Or whatever." My latent social filter finally kicks in, and I bite my lip to keep from embarrassing myself any further.

Señor Smolder asks a simple question, and I manage to launch into a breathless soliloquy, exposing all my dorkiness right out of the gate. But maybe he has a thing for dorky girls because he just smiles.

"Okay, who are you, and where did you come from?" he asks. (I've been wondering that my entire life. Get in line, pal.)

"I'm from Bodeen," I confess. "I know, not cool, but—"

"As in the tiny hick town?" he asks.

No, as in the thriving metropolis of all things awesome.

"Yeah, but I'm just working at this stupid barbecue place to save for college," I explain. The more I tell my 'official story,' the more it feels true. Sometimes, when I'm hanging out in Austin, I actually forget that I still live in Crapville and attend Crapville High. Especially when flirting with a boy like SS. Wait—oh, my God. Is this flirting? I think it might be. I'm having a flirting breakthrough. Sweet Jesus, hallelujah! The curse is over!

But before SS and I can get into the nitty-gritty of our gettin'-to-know-ya chitchat, a guy's voice calls from the backyard.

"Oliver! Get your skinny ass out here! Eddie's guitar is in your trunk!" Oliver turns back to me.

"Hey. What are you doing in approximately three minutes?" he asks.

"Hmm . . . no plans," I offer.

"Cool. Meet you back here."

"Sure," I say. And with that, he turns and dashes out of the room.

Oliver! His name is Oliver! I love him already.

The Worst Timing Ever

I sprint to the bathroom to pee, swipe my pits with some borrowed stink-patrol (gross, but I'm desperate, so don't judge), and apply just a dash of not-trying-too-hard lip gloss before meeting my dream date back at the stereo. While I'm not really down with the whole "nice to meet you, want a blow job?" mating ritual that seems to define all Bodeen High romances, my heart is beating jackrabbit fast. Just the thought of Oliver has my bra practically undoing itself.

In an effort to avoid any spontaneous slutting out, I give myself a stern look in the mirror. "You can make out with him, but *that's it*," I tell my boy-crazed reflection.

"Who are you, my mother?" retorts a familiar, if drunk, voice from behind the shower curtain. I turn and yank back the curtain to find Pash in the arms of a skinny Mohawk boy (of course).

"Babe Ruthless!" she shouts, throwing her drunken arms open wide. "There you are!" Her hair's a mess, she's got lipstick smeared up one cheek, and her bra is hanging out of her back pocket.

"Savage and I were looking everywhere for you," she says, waving to the equally disheveled boy, who has an identical lipstick smear on his cheek. "But now we're going to the store because we have the munchies, and Savage wants some beef jerky."

Savage? His name is Savage? The boy's so skinny even I could take him in a street fight.

"Do you have any idea how much I looooooooove you? You're the best friend ever!" Pash yells, as though she were trying to chat with me from two towns over. Only, I am standing right in front of her as my eardrums take a beating.

"You are seriously blotto, and there's no way you are driving," I say, snatching the keys out of Pash's hands.

"Not me—you. Because you are my best friend, and I loooove you, and I drive you everywhere, so now you can drive me."

Pash stumbles out of the bathtub and into my arms. She can barely stand, and Savage is no use in the helping-me-hold-up-my-drunk-best-friend department. It is at this moment that Pash's face runs through a quick color

wheel of hues before landing on a not-so-healthy-lookin'
green. I know what comes next.

I quickly spin her toward the toilet, throw open the
lid, and try not to be grossed out as the poor girl pukes
her guts out. The same cannot be said for Savage. He
raises his arms in surrender.

"I'm out," he says as he steps over Pash and makes
his exit. Pash catches her breath and looks up.

"I guess when you puke in front of a guy, the relationship's over." She sighs.

"I think, when his name is Savage, it never began,"
I add.

Pash laughs and starts puking again. All I want to do
is get back so I can hang out with Oliver, but somehow
the idea of letting go of my best friend's hair while she's
throwing up in order to hook up with a boy (even though
he's crazy hot) strikes me as evil to the core. I'm only evil
in a superficial way—I can't sink that low.

I cross my fingers and toes, hoping Oliver will wait, but
by the time I take care of Pash and get back to the party,
there's no sign of him. And trust me, I do a full-on FBI missing persons search all over that house, covering the dark-
est reaches of the back and front yards. Alas, no Oliver.

However, I manage to glean some key facts about my
elusive subject. Oliver's nineteen, known as a total sweet-
heart among the Derby Girls, and he just so happens to
be the bassist for a band called the Stats, local up-and-

comers whom Emma describes as "the greatest band ever, if you're into that whole emo, skinny-boy, rocker thing." I am, I admit it.

When Pash and I finally crash at 5:33 A.M. on Rocktavia's living room floor, with only a single blanket and a tiny throw pillow between us, she keeps asking if I hate her.

"Do you hate me? Do you hate me for getting wasted?"

"No," I say, teasingly. "I hate you for getting wasted and not sharing with me."

"I'm a crappy best friend," she whines.

"True, but you probably saved me from a gorgeous boy who could break my heart six ways to Sunday."

"Sounds hot," she whispers, on the verge of sleep.

"Ridiculously." I sigh, before finally dozing off myself.

91

The Stink of Pink

When the Pashmobile finally drops me off the next morning or afternoon or whatever time it is, I am beyond exhausted. The sun burns my tired eyes like a freshly chlorinated pool, and it takes every ounce of energy I have to walk to the front door. I'd rather crawl.

I just want to shower, fall into bed, and sleep forever—not only for the much-needed shut-eye, but for the Oliver dreams I know await me. (I'd be lying if I didn't say I was looking forward to it.)

I take exactly one step into my bedroom before realizing larger forces (literally) have been working against my grand plans for a lazy Sunday afternoon. There is a pink suit hanging from my closet door. I repeat: There is a pink suit hanging from my closet door. A little pink jacket with a little pink skirt, set off by a trio of pink rhinestone buttons.

Here's the deal. I. Don't. Wear. Pink.

No sooner does my stomach start to churn at this color invasion of my personal space than I see Brooke standing in the doorway wearing *the exact same suit.*

"*There* you are!" she sings. "I was just about to phone up Pash's mom and see what was takin' you so long. We don't want to be late."

"For?" I ask, clueless to what this pink-suit–conspiracy thing is all about.

"I'm supposed to believe you forgot about the Miss Bluebonnet Mother / Daughter Brunch," Brooke says, her hand on her pink hip.

Shit! The Mother / Daughter Brunch from Hell that sounded so scary I immediately put it out of my mind? That thing is today? Like, right now? At the exact moment I need some sleep and alone time with my Oliver thoughts? Dear God, thanks for hating me. You suck. Love, Bliss.

"I didn't forget," I manage to choke out.

"Good. You didn't have a stitch to wear, so I thought I'd surprise you," Brooke says, holding the pink suit up to me. "You're welcome," she says, before leaving my room.

Sometimes I feel like I'm just a supporting player in the movie starring Brooke. The script was written way before I showed up, and anything I do that deviates from the story just gets ignored. Of course, I've been miscast in the role of the eldest of two pageant prodigies, but Brooke doesn't care. The show must go on.

And it is this philosophy that finds me half an hour later standing in the living room wearing the dreaded pink suit. (I'm pretty sure that, twenty years from now, when I'm in a therapist's office suffering a total mental breakdown, all my problems will be traced back to this exact moment. This moment will cost me a lot of money.)

Oh, and for all you pink lovers out there, don't take it personally that I hate your favorite hue. I have my reasons. For instance, there are girls who are so fierce that wearing pink makes them look that much cooler (especially when paired with black-and-white-striped tights or a skull choker). On those badass vixens, pink becomes an in-your-face dare that says "hey, world, even in the girliest of colors, I'm still cool as hell, so don't fuck with me." But I, Bliss Cavendar, am not one of those girls. I'm so uncool that even if I were covered in the toughest tattoos, just a touch of pink would still make me look like a rah-rah cheerleader. I need all the black I can get.

Hence the silent scream I feel as I enter the living room dressed like a Barbie career girl (not that Barbie even has a career). Brooke gasps in parental triumph.

"Oh, honeybunch, you look sweeter than a Fredericksburg peach! Doesn't she, Earl?"

She turns to Earl, who, for the moment, is in his own movie. In this riveting scene from Earl's life, he has planted his ass, and his undivided attention, on the TV screen as the Dallas Cowboys go head-to-head with the Denver Colts.

I don't know much about football, but when I see one player take his opponent down with a gruesome flying tackle, I can't help but have immediate, newfound respect. Any derby girl worth her skates would kill to throw a block like that.

"Awesome block!" I shout. Wait, did I just say that out loud? In front of my parents? Rewind, erase. Hand quickly goes over mouth.

Too late. Earl stops, turns sloooowly away from the TV, and looks at me.

"Since when did *you* like football?" he says with suspicion and maybe a touch of hope. If Earl suddenly discovered another football fan in the house, it would be like hitting the jackpot in a lottery he never even entered. Don't get me wrong. I'm all for Earl winning the lottery, but not at my expense. I don't want to get his hopes up, so I quickly cover.

"Oh, um, I don't like football," I say. "I just can appreciate the action," I add, stumbling.

"Let's get a move on or we'll be late," Brooke says before the conversation can get any weirder.

And off we go in our matching mother / daughter outfits. Stop laughing—it's not funny. It could happen to you.

The Brunch from Hell

I really hope wherever you are and whatever awful thing you've done in your life (tortured the family cat when you were five, etc.), may your Karmic payback never include going out in public dressed the same as your mother. Nobody deserves that.

I am forced to "mingle" (i.e., observe) and try not to retch as a dozen mother/daughter duos flaunt themselves in the Swan Room of the Bodeen Country Club, which is completely tacky but has delusions of grandeur.

Corbi and her mother, Val, work the room like self-appointed royalty, and everyone seems to *ooh* and *ahh* with their every gesture. It's so gross.

Even my attempt to take cover by the punch bowl gets thwarted when the dynamic duo struts up, all smiles and fake *good lucks*. As Val and Brooke exchange polite conversation (pretending they don't want to kill each other), Corbi just looks at me mouthing "loser" over and over. She's a class act, that Corbi.

Later, we wander through a hall where the Miss Bluebonnet organizers have arranged a "gallery of girls." That's a fancy way of saying they've taken pictures from all the winners throughout the years, blown them up, and put them on easels for all to see.

And then I see my mom's picture. There, in black and white, is a poster-size shot of Brooke's crowning moment. And guess what? Despite the bad '80s fashion and sky-high hairdo, she was gorgeous. I guess she still is, in her own way, when you think about it (I just usually don't because her pushy behavior eclipses her beauty). I'm fixated.

"Mom," I say in awe, "look at you."

"The bigger the hair, the closer to God, we used to say." She sighs, slightly embarrassed.

"Whatev. You're a total hottie!"

"No. That was a long time ago. Now it's yours and Shania's turn."

Okay, so how weird is this? I'm in public, strong-armed into wearing a mother / daughter outfit from hell, which, on the one hand, makes me hate her more than ever; on the other hand, I'm suddenly struck by this sadness I feel for her. Like, it's somehow crystal clear that she lives through her daughters because she doesn't feel so great about herself. And I wonder why I'm only sixteen and it's obvious to me, and she's forty and it's beyond her grasp.

Sure, the whole scenario is funny and weird and annoying, something to angrily protest against, but in the back of my mind, I know one day I will be gone from Bodeen. I will fade into pageant obscurity with this craptacular town in my rearview mirror. I'll be free. But Brooke will still be here, still chasing the best days of her life, the ones that happened when she was sixteen.

You know how you kind of know something, like it's always been there, but not really in focus? And then one day you *really know*—it was in the dark, and now there's a big, fat spotlight on it?

That's how it is with my mom.

It's so sad, I almost start bawling right there in my pink suit. For the remainder of the brunch, I tame my inner snarling and keep the I-hate-you gestures to a minimum: only one annoyed sigh, half an eye roll, and two I didn't-hear-you grunts.

And as a bonus (for a limited time only), I don't even bring up my favorite familial topic—the fact that I still believe I'm adopted. A stellar performance.

School Daze

*I*n an effort to shake off the pink-suit residue and reclaim my personal identity, I wear my favorite thrift-store T-shirt to school the next day: a baseball tee featuring Stryper, circa 1984.

Who's Stryper, you ask? Only the most perfectly awful '80s, Christian, heavy-metal rock band ever. Not that I knew this when I found my beloved T-shirt. I simply swooned over the image of five guys trying to look tough with their big, permed hair, gobs of makeup, and skinny yellow-and-black-striped spandex pants. In short, a fashion disaster of such major proportions that I had to spend the four dollars on the shirt. It makes me so happy to wear it.

Seriously. One day when you're completely bored, depressed, or both, Google Stryper and have yourself a laugh-fest. Guaranteed.

Plus, I love wearing a real old shirt I found for chump change versus a forty-dollar "vintage tee" that Abercrombie & Fitch sells. I mean, c'mon. If you bought it at the mall, it's not vintage. And that's not snobbery. That's just a fact.

Wearing my Stryper shirt keeps me in a good mood, which I need today, as I am quickly tiring of Corbi's bitchy little shtick. Every single time she passes Pash and me in the hall, she has to give us that look, then giggle to her friends in that "I'm so obviously talking about you, and you can't do anything about it" way. It's such a cliché. Do they teach that in Vapid Popular Girl 101? Is it a special seminar in cheerleading camp? I'm all for taking the high road, but one can only ignore such catty behavior for so long. I have the right to suffer through my crappy education without the added harassment of Ms. Pink Sweater Normal constantly vibing me just because I exist. Letting such bitchiness reign condones it.

So, when Pash and I are walking down the hall and Corbi gives us her signature look, I have no choice but to respond. It's not like it was planned, choreographed, or even rehearsed, but just as we pass, my hip takes on a life of its own and—*BAM!*—I knock Corbi derby-style into a row of lockers. The entire hallway falls to a hush as Corbi catches some serious air and lands in stunned silence on the floor.

"Whoops," I say with maximum sarcasm, "I'm such a klutz."

"Ugh! You can't do that to me!" Corbi finally squeals.

"Um. I think she just did," Pash says, coming in with the assist. We blithely continue down the hall, step through the school doors, and savor the little bit of after-school freedom Bodeen has to offer.

Thanks, Stryper T-shirt. I couldn't have done it without ya.

Sometimes God Doesn't Hate Me

When we're at work, Pash tells Bird-man all about the Corbi Hip-Check Episode. Pash does a hilarious slow-mo reenactment of the fall, complete with the facial expressions Corbi emoted as she took the hit. She ran the gamut, from superior-bitchy to shocked-bitchy to embarrassed-bitchy.

Bird-man is so taken with Pash's performance, I can feel his crush-meter tipping in her direction. Good, because I could use the break.

It is at this moment I look out the window and spot a car parked outside. It's lime-green, 1970-something, with a black racing stripe over the hood, and—oh, who cares what kind of car it is. What matters is that Oliver (!) is leaning against it.

Oliver! As in Señor Smolder, as in the yummy rock boy who was totally sort of flirting with me before the romantic mission was thwarted by my pukey best friend.

My jaw drops. I can practically feel my chin hit the floor. I feel like I have to pee and throw up all at once. And yet I've never been happier.

Oliver gives me this wave—oh my God, the best wave you've ever seen in your life—that somehow says, "Hey, I'm here, but I kind of feel like a dork even though I know you know I'm not really a dork." How could you fall in love with someone just by the way he waves? But I'm pretty sure I do.

Despite all the thoughts running through me like juice in a Krazy Straw, I remain quiet. Pash snaps her fingers in front of my face.

"Your shift is now over. I'm covering for you. Go," she says, shoving me toward the door. "And call me later."

I can hear Bird-man protesting as I walk to the door.

"So, what? That guy shows up here with his cool car, and we just let her go with him?"

"Don't worry your pretty little head about it," Pash tells him.

"But what if he's dangerous?" Bird-man protests.

"Duh. That's kind of the point," Pash says. I love her.

I step out of the Oink Joint and walk toward Oliver. The painfully perfect forever it takes me to cross the parking lot, he stands there watching. I concentrate so hard on traversing the asphalt without tripping, falling, dropping my bag, or any other romance-ending display of public humiliation that I forget to think of anything to say when we are actually standing face-to-face, which we suddenly are.

Not that I can look him in the face. My heart is beating way too fast. I'm too nervous to look at him directly, so my eyes wander to his threadbare T-shirt. There's a hole in the seam near his shoulder, revealing a sliver of pale skin and a single freckle. I suddenly feel the urge to kiss, bite, and nibble that piece of skin taunting me with its yumminess. I want to move in, colonize, and live the rest of my life on that adorable little freckle.

I quickly move my gaze to his shoes before I cause a scene. Or at least I try to. But that Oliver is a tricky one. He manages to catch my eye and half laughs, like, "Hey, isn't this a funny coincidence except for it's not because there's no way in hell anyone in their right mind would ever end up in Bodeen, but let's just pretend it is."

We start to talk. Well, sort of. I know, on paper it looks like the single-dumbest conversation in the history of all conversations, but I assure you the mental dialogue between us is profound.

OLIVER: So . . .
BLISS: So . . . (tucks her hair behind her ear like a dork)
OLIVER: Umm . . . (smiles dreamily)

BLISS: Yeah.

OLIVER: I, uh . . . (shoves his hands in his pockets)

BLISS: Are you, umm, stalking me?

OLIVER: No. Maybe, sort of. Do you mind?

BLISS: No. I kind of always wanted my own stalker.

We laugh the way you laugh at your favorite joke, when all someone has to do is mention the punch line and you're off and running. It's scary, but it's also so comfortable.

Eventually our convo segues to a more direct line of questioning. He looks at my shirt. "Are you really wearing a Stryper shirt?" he says with impressed excitement.

"Wait," I say, suspiciously. "Don't even act like you know who Stryper is." I mean, sure, he's hot, but this shirt is a private joke between me & me. Oliver doesn't get to just show up and carve off a piece for himself. Does he?

He looks me right in the eye and says, with taunting intelligence, "Stryper—'80s, Christian heavy-metal band. Their lyrics were bad, and clearly their fashion choices have survived only for your ironic amusement. But, for the record, their guitarist—Oz Fox—that dude could shred."

Oliver gives me a wicked grin, opens the door of his car, and says, "Hop in, ironic girl." And right then I know that I will have sex with him.

I mean, not right here, right now, in the Oink Joint parking lot (give me a little credit). But eventually.

Stampede

I've heard tales of urban legends such as these—where a girl gets a ride from a luscious boy in his car—but it has never happened to me personally (woo hoo, inner high five). To mark my girl-rides-with-boy-in-his-car devirginification, I am taking serious notes, quietly cataloguing everything in the car: CDs scattered on the floorboard, an empty bag of Funyuns, an explosion of guitar picks, and a yellowed picture of Siegfried & Roy where someone has written "Oliver, we want to tame you like a tiger" tucked under the passenger visor. It's pretty hilarious.

Oliver has his stereo cranked, playing a homemade mix that bounces between Voxtrot, Be Your Own Pet, early Rolling Stones, the Kinks, and a bunch of stuff so hot off the MP3 press, I've never heard it before.

The windows are down, and the wind tangles my hair into a mess I know I will pay for later, but right now I can't be bothered. I am in his car. It will be worth every second of the three hours it will take to untangle this rat's nest.

One CD catches my eye like a golden egg in an Easter hunt: the Stats.

"Can I borrow this?" I ask, trying to sound casual. Somehow the words come out of my mouth boldly. Not only do I desperately want to hear what his band sounds like, but I am keenly aware that if I borrow a CD, it means eventually I will have to give it back, which means we will have to see each other again. I may not know much about this relationship stuff, but I do know seeing each other again is the key part of it.

"Fine. But if I see it in the used bin at Waterloo, there will be hell to pay." He waves an angry fist like a grumpy old man, and I laugh much harder than I probably should.

I look at his hoodie balled up next to the clutch. It's dark gray, except for orange iron-on letters on the front like some code: 3,585,000.

"So, what's with the numbers?" I ask.

Oliver seems a little embarrassed. "Oh. That's my high score from this random pinball game me and my bandmates always play. It's pretty much the stupidest game ever invented. We're totally obsessed."

"Sounds fun. I mean, I love weird stuff like that."

"Really? Wanna check it out?"

I nod, and Oliver hits the gas.

We cruise into Austin, and Oliver weaves his way to a neighborhood called Hyde Park, where all the houses are great-great-grandparents-old and, quite frankly, awesome. Not like the blah 'burbs of Bodeen.

We park in the postage-stamp-sized lot of Hyde Park Pharmacy. It's a total relic, like something from a *Leave It to Beaver* rerun your dad makes you sit through when he's got control of the remote. There's a soda fountain in the back with a turquoise counter and next to that sits the object of Oliver's entertainment affection: a pinball game called Stampede.

Oliver wasn't kidding. It really is the most awful pinball game ever conceived. Stampede has a tacky old-school Western theme with silly illustrations of cowboys, steers, and horses set off by flashing lights. After several games, I still have no idea what's going on, except I love the feeling of Oliver casually leaning against me as he guides my hands over the buttons to work the flippers at just the right moment.

I hit one perfectly, and the pinball sails into the game's sweet spot. A million lights start blinking, the whole game shakes as the thundering sounds of a thousand horse hooves back a silly cowboy voice that shouts, "Yeeeeeeeehaaaaaaaaw! Storm's a-coming! Stampede!"

The audio assault is so overwhelming I want to hide

under a nearby table. "Oliver! That is the most awful thing I've ever heard," I squeal.

"I know," he says with a wicked laugh. "I want to sample it in one of our songs."

Somehow we manage to waste two hours playing the stupid Stampede game over and over, evidence of how I'll happily suffer just to feel his hands on mine. Plus, it seems like only two seconds have gone by, when I realize I have ten minutes to get to Roller Derby practice.

Ring My Bell

*W*hen Oliver drops me off at the Dollhouse, I'm so nervous that I jump out of his car like a bandit fleeing the scene of a crime. Then it occurs to me that I didn't even say good-bye, so I run back to Oliver's window and poke my head inside.

"So, um, thanks for the ride," I say.

"No prob," he says, looking at me. And not just looking at me, I mean *looking* at me, like he can see right through to my soul.

I can feel my nerves rise, and before I have time to flee again, his yummy lips are on mine. Okay, it's not like I'm the queen bee of kissing skill, but when someone as hot as Oliver gives me a little lip time, I'm a quick study. I make that kiss last—long, lingering, and sweeter than molasses.

That is, until I feel a firm slap on my ass and hear Emma shout "get a room!" She giggles with a few of my teammates as they head inside for practice. Whoops. I got so into my Oliver lip-lock, I completely forgot about the blatant PDA. Oh well. That boy is so worth it.

I enter the practice, high from my first real kiss ever. (Okay, there was that sad attempt to make out with Jeremy, aka Germy, on the seventh-grade band trip to Sea-World, but trust me, the less said about that the better.)

Anyway, I'm so woozy and giddy that my first post-kiss attempt at getting geared up for practice ends with my right knee pad on my left elbow and my right elbow pad on my left knee. I'm a safety hazard.

The girls are ripping on me, laughing as I turn deeper shades of red with each crack. I guess it's sort of hilarious, if you're not me. I don't have that luxury.

Malice rushes in and drops her bag dramatically next to mine. "Ruthless!" she shouts, her derby panties in a total bunch, "What did I tell you about dating boys in bands?"

"What?" I say, genuinely perplexed. Did I miss something?

"Oliver Hastings," Malice says, like she's just discovered the secret fact that illuminates some great, unsolved mystery. "He's in a band!"

"Malice. It's Austin—everyone's in a band," Emma says casually.

"Yeah, but the Stats are, like, a real band, a band that doesn't suck," Malice counters.

"It's cool," I say.

"For him," Malice warns, "not you." I had no idea she was this protective.

"Oliver's so not like that. He's kind of a dork, actually. It's supercute," I say.

"Oh, Lord, here we go," Malice says, looking at all the other girls.

"You know, not every guy who's in a band is a total dick, O Bitter One," Crystal says, rolling her eyes at Malice.

"Really?" Malice says, scanning the twenty-four girls all lacing up their skates. "Everyone here who's ever dated a guy in a band, raise your hand."

All the hands go up.

"Okay. And how many of those guys weren't dicks?"

Every hand but Letha's goes down.

"Letha, dating a trombone player in the UT marching band doesn't count," Malice barks as Letha drops her arm.

Malice folds her arms. "I rest my case."

Crystal smiles. "Right, Malice. You're telling me if Jack White walked in here right now and was all, 'Malice, I'd like you to ring my doorbell,' you'd be, like, 'No thanks, you're in a band'?"

We all look at Malice, who starts to crack under the weight of an imaginary date with Mr. White Stripes himself, her celebrity crush of all crushes.

"Okay, fine," Malice finally admits. "I would ring his doorbell, but I wouldn't go to Kinko's and make flyers for his band's gig on Friday."

"I rest *my* case," Crystal says as everyone laughs their asses off. Even Malice cracks a smile of surrender. She throws her arm around my shoulder and says, "Just look out for yourself, okay?"

"'Kay." I nod. I don't know what she's so worried about. Of all the supposed nightmare stories about dating boys in bands, I promise you, they don't apply to Oliver. He's totally different.

I mean, c'mon, if Oliver were Asshole Extraordinaire, would he come all the way to Bodeen to pick me up? Would he pick me up after practice and drive me all the way back to Bodeen? I doubt it.

Though, upon reentering Suckville, USA, it suddenly occurs to me that I'd rather have Oliver drop me off at the Oink Joint instead of my house. The "Oliver, these are my 'rents. 'Rents, this is my Oliver" introduction will leave me vulnerable to a whole line of questioning I'm not at all prepared to deal with. Not tonight. Things are too good.

But Oliver, the gent, insists on seeing me home in the dark, despite my assurances that "Bodeen doesn't have a crime rate. Fashion crimes—yes. But actual crime crimes—no."

"Whatever," says Oliver. "Everybody knows the weirdest murders always happen in small towns. I got your back."

So, as Oliver's car creeps onto my street, I have him pull into the Gundersons' driveway, four houses down from mine. The Gundersons are an elderly couple who always turn out their lights by seven P.M.—they'll never know we were here.

Oliver puts the car in park and gives me a casual look. "Okay, then, see ya later," he says tauntingly.

"Yeah, later," I say, not moving.

"Get out," he says, turning off the ignition.

"I'm already gone," I say, grabbing his keys.

We pause, look at each other, and then, as if on the same unspoken cue, we totally start making out. And not like a sixth-grade make-out, but, like, *for real*. Oliver slides his hands along my shoulders, sloooowly down my arms, and just as he gets to my wrists, he pushes me back in my seat. He pins me there, looks me in the eye, then calmly leaves a trail of kisses from my collarbone to my ear.

It's electric. My toes curl in my flip-flops, and even though there's technically nothing past first base happening, this is not a PG moment. It's very R, at least in my mind.

Minutes later, when Oliver's car pulls out of the drive-way and I wave woozily from the Gundersons' porch (pretending it's mine), one thought blinks in my brain like a red neon sign:

I.

Want.

Him.

Maestro, a Little Music

*L*ike a cat burglar in some old movie, I carefully open the front door and tiptoe to my bedroom, trying to get safely inside before anyone sees me. I'm still on fire from the hot Oliver kiss, and I know my acting skills aren't enough to snuff out the obvious flames, since I'm supposed to be returning from my "SAT study group" and all.

I hear the distant sounds of Brooke, no doubt with Shania by her side, watching *America's Next Top Model* in the back of the house. So I slip into my room undetected.

I wade through the ever-present pile of clothes on my floor to get to my stereo. I carefully pull the Stats CD out of my bag as though it were a precious gem smuggled from some faraway land, drop it onto the player, and turn up the volume, making sure my head-phones are plugged in, of course.

For a moment, during that little hiccup of silence before the music begins, I start to panic. What if Oliver's band totally sucks? My growing feelings for him are firmly rooted in the assumption that I will like his band. What if I don't? What if they sound like some Disneyfied monstrosity created by pods in a lab for vapid mall girls who wouldn't know real music if it hit them upside the head?

Music is pretty much my religion. There's no way I could worship something that made me retch. No. Freakin'. Way. Then again, Oliver is a damn good kisser.

Okay fine. I won't fall in love with him. I'll just make out with him.

The music kicks in, and thank God, it's not an atroc-ity. The Stats are quite good, actually. Honestly, I hate describing bands, because I always feel like I say the same thing over and over, and I never make the music sound as cool as it really is anyway. What's the point? Music is its own language.

But, just so you don't think I'm holding out, the Stats are stripped down, classic garage rock, with catchy gui-tar hooks and a touch of light melody here and there. Not girly but not overly aggro for aggro's sake. They're 84 percent messy loud, and 16 percent sweet geekiness, which is good enough for me.

It's the sixth track that really kicks my music-lovin' ass, a killer tune called "If We Kill Ourselves, Can We Still Hang Out?"

The lyrics follow this total fucked-up guy who hates the world and wants to kill himself. Then he meets this equally fucked-up chick and they make suicide plans together, but while they're hating the world and planning their funerals, he ends up falling for her. Plus, it showcases some awesome moments of Oliver on bass.

It's completely sarcastic and loud and hilarious, but then this bittersweet lyric creeps in at the end:

The most alive I've felt is planning my death with you.

It gives me chills, and I immediately bestow it with the prestigious honor of my new favorite song and stay up listening to it a hundred times in a row as a show of good faith.

I study the Stats' understated DIY CD cover—no fancy booklet or liner notes, they're a total starter band—featuring a grainy Polaroid of Oliver and his three band mates sitting on a granny sofa in the back of a pickup truck. Brilliant.

I flip it over and read the credits on the back. There are a few names mentioned, but my eyes only go to one, "Oliver Hastings: Bass."

Oliver Hastings: Bass, Oliver Hastings: Bass, Oliver Hastings: Bass, Oliver Hastings: Bass.

Question: Could School Be More Boring? Answer: No

So, Pash and I sit in Mr. Smiley's class as he drones on about supply-side economic philosophies, and who am I kidding—I'm practically asleep. Head on desk, *this close* to having a little puddle of drool next to my mouth. That's what happens when I'm beyond exhausted. No snoring, just drool, but usually on my pillow in the safety and comfort of my own home. Not in public.

As Mr. Smiley lectures about our six-week project and how we should get with our partners and "shake a tail-feather sooner than later" (Mr. Smiley-speak for "get crackin'"), Pash whispers to me, "He's talking about you, slacker."

"You know I'm a procrastinista," I say, not lifting my head from my desk. "But I'll get it done." I could do without the judgmental look I can feel Pash giving me as I close my eyes. Who does she think she is? Last time I checked, she's not the only one rockin' the honor roll these days.

Besides, I really need her to listen to the Stats right now. It would be unfair for me to keep Oliver's band to myself.

"Listen," I say, covertly passing her one of my iPod earphones. "Isn't this the best song ever?"

Before Pash can settle in to the sweet tunes, an office aide enters and slips Mr. Smiley an official note. He reads the note, then waves the telltale yellow paper in my direction.

"Sunflower, you got yourself a date with destiny," Yoda-man says before handing me the slip and sending me on my way.

You Can Bee All That You Want to Bee

I wander into the main office, flash my yellow note, and am quickly ushered like a VIP toward Ms. Meyers's office. Ms. Meyers is our school's guidance counselor, who neither guides nor counsels. Not that she doesn't try.

Ms. Meyers is really into slogans. Her favorite is "You can bee all that you want to bee"—an affirmation she likes to drive home by pointing at a piece of bumblebee jewelry that she always wears. *Par example.* I'll be walking innocently down the hall, trying not to be noticed, when Ms. Meyers will get me in her crosshairs.

"Good morning, Bliss. How are you?" she'll say.

"I'm fine, Ms. Meyers," I'll answer.

"Good. Don't forget, Bliss. You can *bee*"—points to bumblebee ring—"all that you want to *bee*"—points to bumblebee earring. It's like a shtick she developed in a previous life as motivational speaker for six-year-olds on a low-budget children's show, only the gig didn't pan out and, thanks to the miracle of a couple well-chosen community-college courses, Ms. Meyers now plies her trade to high-schoolers. And, naturally, she brought her bee wisdom with her. Lucky us.

The woman has no shortage of bee accoutrements. You name it, Ms. Meyers has got it—bumblebee rings, bumblebee pins, bumblebee earrings, bumblebee necklaces, and sometimes she wears them all at once. Today Ms. Meyers is showing real restraint, with only a single, bedazzled bumblebee pin perched on her shoulder, its rhinestone wings wide open, as though the bee had just flown in through the window and landed there. It's pretty awesome as bad fashion statements go. I'd probably hail its genius even more if Ms. Meyers weren't so annoying.

She talks reeeeeaaaallly slooow, overenunciating everything. Plus, she's the kind of counselor who's really into hanging motivational posters all over her office. Y'know, the kind of über-positive, uplifting propaganda that is meant to keep teenagers from taking drugs and getting knocked up. But, honestly, the posters are so obnoxious, I'm tempted to get pregnant, start shooting heroin, and join a gang just to protest.

Anyway, Ms. Meyers is always trying to get us to "learn something" about ourselves in her office. Despite her zero success rate on that front so far, I must confess I did actually learn something about myself today. I learned that nothing engages my gag reflex like walking into her office and seeing my parents sitting there.

Oh, yeah. I open the door, and there they are: Brooke and Earl Cavendar, sitting side by side.

What the—? Who invited them? Now, I don't know why I've been summoned to Ms. Meyers's office, but I assure you, whatever this is about, we do not need to bring parents into it. *Mom, Dad, just quietly go to your car and forget you were ever here. Ms. Meyers and I can handle it on our own.*

If only. I can already see that my mother is on high makeup alert, which is never a good sign. Granted, Brooke routinely piles on so much Mary Kay, it's difficult to tell what high alert is—for the untrained eye. But I know. The more nervous or upset she is, the more makeup she's wearing.

"Never go into battle without your armor on," she likes to say.

Ms. Meyers looks at me and smiles. "Hi, Bli-iss. Come on inn and haave a seeaaat."

But Brooke cuts to the chase, staring daggers through her Tammy Faye lashes. "Bliss Cavendar, tell me you did not shove Corbi Booth into a locker yesterday," she says.

"Oh, that," I say. *Duh, I should have known that's why I'm here.*

Before I can explain, Ms. Meyers folds her hands on her desk and says, "Corbi has an enormous bruise on the back of her leg."

"And she has to cheer tonight!" my mom adds in a panic, as if the very idea of Corbi Booth having a bruise on her leg is a sign of the cheerleading apocalypse, like the world order of pom-poms will come down on Brooke for having spawned the child who started it. Whatever.

"So," I say, "cancel the game."

"Bliss Cavendar!" my mother says, nearly jumping out of her chair. And then I start to get a little pissed—no, really pissed. My mother couldn't care less about me and my side of the story. All she cares about is Corbi.

"Look, I know Corbi's Little Miss Rah-Rah Perfect to y'all. But, for the record, when you're not looking, she's pretty evil. I'm not taking it anymore."

Ms. Meyers tilts her head and keeps her voice annoyingly calm. "It's ooookaaay to be aaaangry, Bliss, but what concerns me is how you deal with your anger."

Maybe it's the Babe Ruthless in me, but before I can censor myself, the phrase "I think I dealt with my anger just fine" comes out of my mouth.

The ever-silent Earl starts to chuckle in a way that lets me know that underneath the "united parental front," he just might be on my side, after all. (Go, Earl!) But Brooke immediately shuts him down with a look of death.

In the end, Ms. Meyers is not equipped to deal with the slippery truths of high school bully-bitches and the wallflowers who unexpectedly challenge their power. So she quickly wraps up the meeting. I promise to be less of a klutz, and Ms. Meyers reminds me to "bee all I can bee" before sending me back to class.

Frock 'n' Roll

*I*n light of the shame and humiliation Corbi-gate has brought upon my entire family (translation: Brooke and Brooke only), I am forced to do some swift penance to keep my mom from engaging in full freak-out mode. This is why I am currently standing in Clara's Sewing Stop being fitted for a custom Miss Bluebonnet gown instead of hanging out with Oliver. Talk about torture.

Don't get me wrong. I love the idea of custom-made clothes. I mean, I would really love it if I were in Paris, Milan, or anything remotely resembling one of the world's fashion capitals. Bodeen, Texas, however, is hardly the hub of haute couture.

But don't tell Clara that. When it comes to proms and brides, anyone who's anyone in Bastrop County goes to Clara's for her frock. And her pageant gowns? Well, my friends, those are the stuff of legend.

"Pageants are the canvas for my art," Clara likes to say.

And right now I'm wearing the muslin mock-up of what in six weeks is "guaranteed" to have me waltzing in the winner's circle. The skirt is so huge you could hide a small car beneath it. Brooke stands behind me, prodding and pulling the muslin into a perfect fit, as Clara pins it in.

"Oh, Clara, the silhouette is just lovely." Brooke sighs, tilting her head as she watches me in the mirror.

My survival tactic for this moment is to take a little vacation in my head, thinking about Oliver. And that kiss, that crazy-perfect kiss in the car with his hands on my wrists. It hasn't left my mind—not even for a second—since it happened. In class, when I'm chewing on a pen, I feel him kissing me. Walking through the cafeteria line at school, I see him kissing me. Trying on this pageant dress, I taste him kissing me.

"Now, if we could just nip in this waist here." Brook pulls the bodice so tight I feel my ribs fighting for their life.

"Mom," I say, gasping out of my Oliver daydream, "I can't breathe."

"Sure you can. Now, just one more thing," she says, ignoring my plea for oxygen. She whips out a pair of silicone breast enhancers, then stuffs them down the front of the strapless gown.

"Aaarrgh!" I say, mortified. "You're totally molesting me!"

"It's for a good cause." Good cause? What the hell is she talking about, "good cause"? Is she planning on donating my Miss Bluebonnet crown to the victims of natural disasters? *Now, bless y'all's hearts, I know that awful storm destroyed your lives and made you homeless and whatnot, but here you go. Here's a rhinestone crown to help get you through.* Good cause, my ass.

I catch a glimpse of my reflection. The waist is pulled so tight and my boobs suddenly look inflated—I've been Barbiefied against my will.

"No," I declare. "I am not wearing stunt boobs."

"Oh, honeybunch, I'm not sayin' your little nuggets aren't darlin'. They are—in daily life. But this is not daily life. This is Miss Bluebonnet, and we need the ta-da."

Are you paying attention to this? My mother not only just publicly felt me up, but she then referred to my breasts as "little nuggets." Lovely.

Live it up, Shania, as you skip around playing with your fairy wand. One day it's gonna be you up here.

An hour later, when the bonding train chugs on over to Wal-Mart for some prime-time grocery shopping, we bump into Corbi and Val. Perfect. Just perfect.

"Well, look who it is!" Val says, rounding the corner with her basket. "How're y'all doin'?" Val has a way of making the sweetest phrase sound like she's drawing a sword.

"Oh, we're busy, busy, busy! Just got back from Clara's for Bliss's dress fitting," Brooke says, trying to brag.

The primal competitiveness simmering beneath Brooke and Val's sugary exchanges turns up a notch.

"Oh. Y'all are still doin' Clara's—that's so . . . adorable. We just got back from Houston. For Corbi's gown."

A silent malfunction happens in Brooke's mind. *I'm sure it never occurred to her to go to the big city.*

"What? Y'all aren't havin' Clara do Corbi's gown?"

"Oh, Brooke. Clara's is fine—for Bodeen. But we're thinkin' bigger than just pageants. Modelin', movies, music, TV. I mean, a big talent agent saw Corbi in Houston, and he said there's no reason why she couldn't have her very own *Laguna Beach*. She's a star in the makin'."

"Wow. Well, that sounds excitin'."

"Sure is," Val gloats. "Well, happy shoppin', y'all!"

"Happy shoppin'!" Brooke smiles through her bitterness.

When Val and Corbi disappear down the cereal aisle, Brooke turns to me, her eyes flickering with competitive concern. "Bliss! What is *Laguna Beach*?" she demands like a squealy preteen on the hunt for the newest, coolest brand of jeans before anyone else discovers them.

Is this what my life has come to? Telling my mom about a shallow MTV show chronicling a bunch of spoiled bitches who steal each other's boyfriends? As much as I'd prefer not to be my mother's pop-culture crutch, I know if I don't produce an answer fast, she'll never shut up about it.

So, I shrug my shoulders and say with utmost serious-ness, "*Laguna Beach* is this reality show about a bunch of super-interesting teenagers who are really deep and smart and just doing their best to make the world a better place."

"Well. If Corbi could be on one of those shows, you could too. You better step it up, Bliss," Brooke says. Her sarcasm detector is clearly malfunctioning today.

The Big O

*I*t feels like a million years later when I finally get to see Oliver again. Okay, so it's only been forty-eight hours, but I'm already addicted and jonesing for a fix.

I'm at Pash's when he and I start a massive IM-a-thon before Pash so selfishly boots me off her PC. (Something about having to do actual homework. Craziness.)

Before the smart-girl interruption, Oliver and I make plans to meet tomorrow. He's gonna pick me up from the Oink Joint at noon so we can go to Austin to hang. There's no delicate way for me to leave school at eleven A.M. without arousing major administrative suspicion (I'd have to have my mom sign me out). So, I decide to just skip the whole day to make the rendezvous worthwhile. All I have to do is bring a sick note the day after

(I've always wanted to put my forgery skills to good use), and we don't have to bring parent/office face time into this transaction. We've had enough of that lately.

When I tell Pash I'm ditching, she gives me THAT look—her signature stare that starts with disapproval and dissolves into complete approval. She's good at that one.

"Does Oliver have a friend?" she asks, only half meaning it, but that half *really means it*.

"Um, maybe," I grunt. I don't want to be selfish, but I sort of want to spend my ditch-day with Oliver alone. At least this one time. But I'm not about to tell her that. I'm hoping she'll back away quietly.

"Oh, forget it," she says. "I'm not gonna be your tag-along. Just . . . if you meet someone you think is right for me—"

"Totally."

To kill time before the Oliver chariot squires me away, I hang out at the Oink Joint, flipping through mags and listening to my iPod. Bird-man gives me this "what are you doing out of school?" look. And I greet him with a silent "it's none of your business—go back to managing" look.

I do kind of have a soft spot for the B-man, but I totally resent how he promotes any and all rebelliousness, but then turns on you if he's not included. Sorry, Bird-man, but you can't come on my date. Deal with it, dude.

It's 12:37 when Oliver comes rollin' in, all sleepy-haired and adorable.

"Am I late?" he asks.

"Nope," I lie.

"Good," he says, pushing the door open from his side of the car. I hop in.

"I'm starving," he says. "How 'bout you?"

"Yeah, but I *don't* recommend the Oink Joint," I say, staring at the air-conditioning vent. I can't look at him without getting nervous all over again. I seriously have to get over that.

"No worries. I got the food thing covered," he says, heading out of town.

I love it when Oliver drives. He's watching the road, and I can steal all the glances I want.

In Austin, we go to the Tamale House and have the best cheap Mexican food ever. We sit on the curb, chucking bits of beef at grackles, greedy little black birds that are a chicer, cooler version of pigeons.

With my grubbing complete, I nudge Oliver. "We should go to a record store," I say.

"Record store," he says, dramatically pondering the suggestion. "Hmm. Okay, I'm all for it."

We head to Waterloo, the original Austin spot for music consumption. As we head inside, Oliver shakes his head. "Man, it's so soulless to get your music online. This is the way real music fans shop."

Inside, the place is covered with concert posters, and music lovers browse with hard-core seriousness.

Oliver nods to the completely gross but surprisingly friendly fat redheaded dude behind the counter.

"Oliver, 'sup?" Fatty asks.

"Same ol', same ol'," Oliver answers.

We go our separate ways, flipping through racks of CDs. At one point, Oliver brushes past when we're in the same aisle. He hooks his finger in the belt loop of my jeans, pulls me back to him, and whispers "you are hot" in my ear before disappearing behind a case of vinyl.

I get so distracted, it takes me several seconds to refocus on my CDs, and when I do, I realize I'm holding a copy of Ashlee Simpson's latest transgression. I quickly put it back and get my hands on a Dead Boys CD, just so I can feel normal again.

Waterloo has a wall of sealed-off listening booths that look like old-school telephone booths you see in '80s movies. You can step inside, shut the door, and sample the music before you buy. Or you can go inside with the boy you skipped school for and pretend to listen to the new Bright Eyes disc while stealing kisses when no one's looking—that's what Oliver and I are up to.

That is, until Oliver finally says, "Wanna get out of here?"

"Totally," I say. As if I have any idea of where we could go.

Movie Make Out 101

*O*liver parks a couple of blocks away from the UT campus and leads me through the grounds like he owns the place. That's one of the best things I'm starting to observe about Oliver. No matter where he goes, he just belongs there. And when I'm with him, I belong there too. He's my passport to all things cooler and more interesting than Bodeen.

We end up at Hogg Auditorium, where all the hipster film students hang out watching old, obscure movies and it costs, like, two dollars to get in. Today, some '60s black-and-white French flick called *Breathless* is on the marquee. Oliver and I sneak in fifteen minutes after it's started, sit at the very back, and pretty much make out the entire time. At least, we attempt to until I have a little grooming confidence meltdown that throws everything into a tailspin.

You see, I'm not the most experienced girl in the world. I'm bound to make a mistake or two (or fifty). Like today. Oliver and I start a no-holds-barred kiss-a-thon (very good), when I suddenly realize I forgot to shave my right leg this morning (very bad). Now, I'm sure you're asking yourself "what kind of half-wit retard forgets to shave one leg?" And, trust me, if I had the answer for that one, I'd be sittin' pretty with two silky-smooth gams, mugging down with this luscious lad without a care in the world.

But, alas, my flawed genetic makeup has a way of thwarting my attempt at a good time. Sometimes I get so busy daydreaming, I forget the little chores I should be tending to, like remembering to shave *both legs* when I'm taking a shower.

As embarrassing luck would have it, Oliver's hand keeps trying to touch my right leg. And I keep moving it away—I don't want to gross him out with my cactus thigh—but his hand is like a man on a mission. The more I move my leg away, the more his hand pursues me. It goes on and on until I'm slouched so low in my seat, I might as well be sitting on the floor.

"What is your deal?" he finally whispers, kind of annoyed.

"Nothing," I say.

"Nothing? You're practically on the floor, you little freak," Oliver says, looking down at me as my ass hovers three inches above the candy-sticky floor. I search and search for some excuse that might make sense, but all I come up with is—

"I just, um, I don't . . . want my leg touched right now. Okay?"

"Oh," Oliver says, and then after a long, uncomfortable pause, "Look. If you don't want be here, I don't want to force it. You don't have to get all weird and sit on the floor."

Oliver sits up and removes his arm from around my shoulder. The minute he takes it away, I feel like I've been thrown into a snowstorm without a coat. It's freezing. It's amazing how fast you can get used to someone's arm embracing you.

I was just trying to spare him the grossness of my unshaved leg, and now he thinks I hate him. My heart sinks and races in the silence until I finally blurt out, "I totally like you. It's justthatI didn'tshavemyrightlegandI didn't want to gross you out, okay?"

Oliver stops and gives me a look.

"What?" he says.

"You heard me," I say. "I forgot to shave. I'm a total Sasquatch leg."

"Wait, you forgot to shave one of your legs?" Oliver laughs. "Man. You are a piece of work."

"Sorry. I know it's gross," I say as he runs his hand over it.

"Ooh. Prickly. That's cool. If my hand itches, I'll just rub on your leg to scratch it for me." He smiles. We're in the dark, but I can already hear what his words sound like when he smiles. I love that.

I like that he makes fun of me—in a good way. I decide that's a very important trait to have in a boy you make out with and secretly hope will officially become your boyfriend.

I had no idea a guy could be this cool about a chick with hairy legs. I expected him to retch and run for the exits. Is that just an Oliver thing, or are all guys that laid-back about this kind of thing? It's weird—nobody tells you that stuff.

Oh, and on the movie front, just so you don't think I'm totally lame, I highly recommend seeing *Breathless,* as it is probably the coolest black-and-white French movie ever made. I can't tell you what the plot is (I was sort of distracted), but it was shot in Paris, and the clothes are to-die-for mod. Trust me. If you have the chance, you should see it for the fashion-gasm alone.

This Is Not My Beautiful Life

*O*n the Roller Derby front, I'm happy to report that after our loss against the Sirens, the Hurl Scouts have been on an undefeated tear. We've taken down the Cherry Bombs, the Black Widows, the Fight Crew, and tonight we get a second chance against the Sirens.

Between Malice's and Emma Geddon's fierce blocking, and Crystal Death's and Babe Ruthless's killer jamming (hello, that would be me), those bad cops didn't know what hit them.

Even Blade can't keep his jackass dance moves in check when I take a hot whip off Emma's mile-long leg to score four points.

"Save it for the after-party, you freak!" Juana Beat'n shouts from the infield as several embarrassed skaters pelt him with empty water bottles. Not that it stops him from cabbage-patching. The dude's got happy feet. Personally, I love Blade's spontaneous bad choreography. Can you imagine any coach in any other sport doing the worm on the infield? Only in Roller Derby, my friends.

I just wish Pash was here to witness the hilarious genius of it all. She's quarantined herself in Bodeen to finish some major science fair project, something too brilliant for my plebian mind to wrap itself around. I guess if she's off finding the cure for cancer, I can't hate on her too much.

Besides, when the Derby Girls take over the Star Seeds Diner after the bout, the best moments are in-jokes and derby references. I'm not sure if Pash would really get it. These girls have definitely become my fam.

Well, all of them except Dinah Might, who has resisted charter membership into the Babe Ruthless Fan Club. She resents me more than ever. To make matters worse, the Hurl Scouts are playing her undefeated Holy Rollers next. All anyone can talk about is how she and I are the "matchup of the season." Great. As if I needed the pressure.

The more I try to be nice to Dinah, the more I can see her internally plotting my death. And I swear it's not just in my head. Last week, we lined up to jam in a scrimmage. I gave Dinah a respectful nod and a friendly smile. She gave me stink-eye and hissed, "Suck my skate, newbie," as the whistle blew. That's her new tactic. Dinah pretends that no matter what I do, no matter how hard I skate, no matter how many times Atom Bomb mentions me in the play-by-play game announcements—to her, I am invisible. Like she can't even be bothered to remember my name.

It's sort of transparent and immature in a kind of Corbi way (same attitude, different blood sport), but I'd be lying if I said it didn't bother me. Corbi's just some cheerleader pageant-skank I couldn't care less about in the long run, but Dinah's an amazing skater, the star of the league, the reason I wanted to play Roller Derby in the first place. It would be nice if she actually acknowledged me. Not that I could complain to anyone about Dinah. She's sacred. Everybody loves her.

I'm not a total slouch, though. Tonight, we're all scattered between five booths in Star Seeds Diner, and Eva Destruction from the Fight Crew stands on a table, holding a rolled-up tube.

"Okay, Chatty Cathys, shut up your pieholes for two seconds! I have an announcement. As your official poster bitch, I present you with the latest and greatest for our next bout," she says.

I watch as Eva unrolls the poster, once again sharing her graphic brilliance with us. As always, it's cooler than cool, but something seems off. The girl in the poster—she has familiar legs, arms I recognize—and then, *Oh, shit! That's not Dinah on the poster. That's . . . me!*

Everyone cheers, and Malice chucks an onion ring at me. "Hell, yeah, short stuff!" she shouts.

I wish I could say I feel an internal high-five, yay-me moment, but two thoughts immediately override the celebration.

One: Out of the corner of my eye, I see Dinah two booths back nearly choke on a fry when the poster is revealed. I have no doubt she will try to kill me next week.

And two: All I can think is, *My mother must never see this poster.* I don't know why—it's not like Brooke frequents the Austin tattoo shops, pizza dives, and coffeehouses that display Eva's fine work—but a flock of butterflies fly from the bottom of my stomach to the back of my throat.

It isn't until I'm alone in my bedroom the next day that I actually look at the copy Eva gave me. Okay, I confess, it's pretty freakin' awesome. I break out in a little personal happy dance. *Miss Bluebonnet can have her billboard. I'm a Roller Derby poster girl!*

I hear my mom coming down the hall and quickly slip the poster under my mattress, where it shall remain undetected.

When BFFs Attack

So, Pash and I are creating sculpture—like we always do—with our rehydrated, school-lunch mashed potatoes, and I'm telling her how I don't care what cancer cure she's trying to invent, but she has to swear right now, on all things that are unholy, she will be at the next bout.

Not only do I want her rooting me on, I want a witness to tell my parents what went down in case I die at the hands of Dinah. And that I loved them, despite all the misunderstandings and bad music and fashion they tried to force on me.

You would think a best friend would be cool about these things, have your back. Not Pash. Not these days. It's like she's constantly pissed off at me for nothing. Which is so not Pash.

And, ohmygod, I never should have even said a word about being the poster girl. Her mood immediately darkened upon hearing that one. She didn't say "Bliss, that's so cool" or "awesome—I can't wait to see it." No. My great news was met with a storm cloud brewing above her head.

"Guess what I did yesterday?" Pash asks, confrontationally. It suddenly occurs to me that Pash's eyeliner is different. Not the color, but the angle. Very cat-eye; it's hot.

"You changed your eyeliner," I say.

"Yeah, like, two weeks ago," she deadpans, and I feel like a speck of mud. "And yesterday, I went to Wal-Mart and . . . picked up a few things," she says.

"What? You five-fingered without me? Pash! That's an us thing, not a solo thing," I practically shout.

"Well," she says, "when there's no us around, I guess I have to go solo."

"I'm sorry, okay? I owe you some good hang-out time. Just promise me you're coming to the bout this weekend. There's gonna be a really great party. We're gonna have an epic time." Parties are Pash's weak spot. She can't say no.

"Fine, but you can't make out with Oliver in some dark corner the whole time."

"Okay," I agree.

Between you and me, I'm getting the jealousy vibe with a capital J. And it's not like I want to call her on it. I don't want Pash to feel bad that we don't hang out as much anymore. But, for the record, I did try to get her to join Roller Derby with me. I begged, and she said no. She can't blame me for having fun without her.

However. If I were stuck in Hickville 24/7 and my best friend got a boyfriend (BFGBF), I'd be hatin' life too. And I sure as hell would not want the best friend in question accusing me of being jealous. So, for now, I'll let it lie.

This weekend's gonna rock. Provided I survive the bout.

Hurl Scouts vs. Holy Rollers

*S*aturday night. An hour before the highly anticipated showdown between the Hurl Scouts and the Holy Rollers, Malice skates backstage.

"Holy shit. It's crazy packed out there!" she says.

"You ready, poster girl?" Emma says, turning to me.

"Yep," I lie, lacing up my Reidells. I haven't put one skate on the track, but already I feel the beads of sweat taking shape on my upper lip.

Atom Bomb announces our team's roster, then finishes with "And last but not least, the rookie upstart, number forty-eight . . . Baaaaaaabe Ruuuuuuthlesss!"

The crowd roars so loud, the noise nearly knocks me off my skates. Technically, derby girls should look fierce and badass at all times, but I can't help smiling like a dope hearing all those people cheer.

Of course, when the Holy Rollers hit the track for their skate out, Dinah gets the same reception. Maybe more, but so what? I'm not scared off. Not tonight. I catch a glimpse of Oliver and Pash in the audience and think, *I can rock this. Dinah who?*

The place falls to an electric hush as Dinah and I line up for our first jam. She gives me a cold sneer. I just smile. The first whistle blows, and the pack of blockers takes off. The second whistle rattles in its little metal cage, and Dinah and I shoot out like synchronized bottle rockets.

Going into the first turn, I'm half a step ahead, cutting, ducking, and dodging through the pack. I have the lead. I skate hard, leaning into the track and crossing over to get full speed. I suddenly hear the crowd roar as Dinah sneaks past me from behind.

Dinah gets into the pack first, passing three of my blockers for three points. Even though I'm half a step behind, I pass three of her blockers—we're tied at three points each.

Dinah gets the first points, but she also gets called for an elbowing penalty against Malice, so she has to spend the next jam in the penalty box. With Dinah out, I'm jamming against the Holy Rollers' Ella Mental. Ella's a sweet girl, but jamming against her is like taking candy from a baby.

Poor Ella doesn't know what hit her when, a minute later, I lap the pack twice, racking up six points. The crowd goes wild.

For the briefest moment, I'm bummed that my parents aren't here. Of course Roller Derby is not and never will be Brooke's thing, but it would be cool for her to witness one thing I'm not a total loser at.

I mean, there's a cheering crowd. Couldn't she at least respect that? Sort of?

When Dinah gets out of the penalty box, she's like a just-released convict looking to settle the score. The Holy Rollers may have God on their side, but the Hurl Scouts aren't about to crumble. We hold them off. And not just me—my entire team.

During a time-out huddle on the infield, Malice offers five little words of wisdom: "We can beat those bitches!"

To which we reply, "Hell, ya!" And we believe it.

The more we believe it, the better we skate. The better we skate, the more the Holy Rollers get nervous. The more they get nervous, the more they fall apart. I'm sure that adds up to some sophisticated Mr. Smiley economic theory, but as I look at the score blinking "Holy Rollers, 9, Hurl Scouts, 16," I think it's pretty simple. It's a plain-ol' Texas ass whuppin'. Yee freakin' haw.

We're a few jams away from halftime, and I can feel Dinah's desperation. She's bringing all she has to even the score before halftime.

We line up to jam, when all of a sudden, men in bright yellow coats suddenly dot the crowd. They swiftly make their way from the back of the audience to the front. Within seconds, the mysterious gang of yellow-coat dudes surrounds the track.

I have no idea what the hell is going on, but I know it can't be good when I hear Atom Bomb go from his usual crowd-baiting "folks, we got ourselves a battle royale tonight!" to an abrupt "oh, shit."

I look to Emma, who's already un-Velcro-ing her wrist guards. "Damn fire marshal," she says.

A minute later I get a crash course in the world of fire-marshaldom. Apparently, there's a whole arm of the law dedicated to overseeing crowd capacity. Turns out the reason the Dollhouse feels so packed tonight is because it is. We have three hundred more people than is legally allowed. It's a derby bust.

So, just as our adrenaline is kicking into high gear, our bout is shut down. We go from being on the verge of beating the undefeated Holy Rollers to being hastily thrown out of the Dollhouse. Either that or face arrest. And they ain't kiddin'.

I still have my skates on as I ride the wave of people out the door. Outside it's mayhem, and there are cops everywhere.

A couple of angry guys yell at the cops as they leave: "Roller Derby is not a crime, man!" which would make me laugh if I weren't already freaked by all the police-folk hovering around.

I don't see Oliver or Pash anywhere. When I turn, I see Malice, Dinah, and all the other captains against the wall being questioned by police.

"Malice!" I shout out of concern.

"It's cool, Ruthless. Just meet us at the party!" she shouts back.

I turn and suddenly find myself face-to-face with the barrel chest and burly biceps of a midnight-blue uniform and a shiny badge. I tilt my head up to see the scariest cop face on the planet glaring down at me. I nearly pee. Thankfully, I manage to keep it under control.

"I'm gonna need to see your ID," Officer Power Trip says.

"What?" I say, having an internal freak-out.

"Young lady, you can either show me your ID or you can go to jail," Officer PT says as he runs his fingers over the handcuffs tucked into his belt for dramatic effect. As if I needed that.

Trust me. I'm scared enough. Can you imagine the phone call to Brooke if I got arrested playing Roller Derby? Me either.

I'm praying as I dig into my bag and hand him the only thing I have, my high school ID. Officer PT looks it over, shines a flashlight in my eyes (thanks, dude), then asks, "Is this all you've got?"

"Yes," I say, before adding, "sir. Yes, sir."

"You're only sixteen years old?" he says. Is that necessary, to say it out loud? Here is not the place to be broadcasting my age!

"Yes, sir," I quickly answer, hoping we can move on to a less incendiary line of questioning.

"Well, Ms. Cavendar, don't you think you're a little young to be running with this crowd?" Again with the age.

I want to tell him to kiss my ass, he doesn't know me, this is the best crowd I've ever had the pleasure of running with. But I don't want to go to jail or cause a scene where all my derby sisters suddenly find out I'm not exactly eighteen. So . . .

"Yes, sir. That's why I'm leaving right now, sir. So I can get home. Sir." The *sir*s may be overkill, but I can tell Officer Power Trip loves it. Every time I say sir his badge shines a little bit brighter.

"All right," he finally says. "I'll let you go. But you do understand you are an accomplice if y'all violate the fire marshal code again."

"Yes, sir." I nod.

"You're free to go," he says, handing me back my school ID. As I reenter the fray of the thinning crowd, an arm slips around my waist.

"There you are!" Oliver says. "Man. That was the best bout ever! Too bad it got shut down."

"Totally. Have you seen Pash?"

"Nah. We'll catch up with her at the party. C'mon," he says, pulling me toward his car. Normally I would stay and wait for Pash to rear her stylish little head, but when I look up and see news helicopters arriving on the scene, I know it's time to flee. I already dodged one parental-notification bullet. I don't want to risk any further outing of myself tonight.

I grab Oliver's cell and text Pash: LUZR! WHR R U? GON 2 PRTAY - SI U THR. PS - NO MOHOX 4 U 2NIT, DRNK GRL!

I'm in a bit of a cell-phone drought at the moment (I lost four of them in three months, so my mother cut me off from the digital revolution), thus I depend on the kindness of cell-phone-lending strangers / boyfriends.

No Fire Marshals Here

In light of the fire marshal crackdown, the party vibe starts on a bummed-out note. However, when we see the derby bust covered on the evening news, everyone quickly shifts into full celebratory mode. It feels a little bit dangerous and criminal, like the glory of having a tattoo without suffering through the pain of a needle.

Plus, everyone's so stoked about the near undoing of the Holy Rollers, the team captains are holding an impromptu meeting by the keg, discussing the possibilities of a rematch.

For the first hour, I check Oliver's phone over and over to see if Pash texted me back. By the second hour, I give up. She must have just driven back to Bodeen. That nut. I can't believe she's missing all this fun.

Oliver and his older brother, Hank, a lush lad in his own right (proof that their family tree is ripe with hotties), get out their guitars and serenade us with an impromptu unplugged session on the back porch. Hank is the twenty-four-year-old lead singer and songwriter for the Stats (i.e., he gets all the girl action). Oliver's happy to hang back, staring at his shoes and strumming his bass while his hair falls in his eyes. Hank may be the obvious choice, but I'd take Oliver any day, which kind of works in my favor, considering I already have him.

At some point after one, Oliver and I end up in Rocktavia's bedroom, talking and taking turns playing DJ on her stereo. We're sitting on the floor, lazily hitting each other with pillows as we talk about stuff, but mostly bands. Out of nowhere he goes, "Guess what?"

"What?" I ask.

"We're going on tour," he says, "with the Benedicts." My eyes suddenly get bigger than dinner plates. The Benedicts are pretty much the coolest indie-rock band in Austin. Even if you haven't heard of them, you would totally recognize their music. Trust me. They're the bee's knees.

"No way!" I squeal, not because I'm the squealy type, but because that's how the unfiltered excitement comes out of me (I'm a dork). "That's so freakin' cool! Seriously, that's the coolest thing that's ever happened to anyone I know. You could not be any cooler if you—"

"Bliss," Oliver interrupts.

"Yeah?"

"You have to stop saying *cool.*" I nod, and then think better of it.

"Cool, cool, cool, cool, cool, cool, cool," I say, until Oliver puts his hand over my mouth to shut me up. I bite his hand, and he laughs.

"When are you going?" I ask. I suddenly have this fantasy of Oliver and his band hitting the road in a big tour bus in summer, with me coming to visit him in different cities. My mind hopscotches all over the country, picturing various clubs, with Oliver playing onstage and me watching from the back (wearing some killer vintage dress, of course). He'll wave at me between songs, and I'll roll my embarrassed eyes back at him, secretly loving it all. Hmm . . . yeah, I think I like this tour thing.

"We leave Monday," Oliver says.

"Muh-what?" I choke. That's waaaay too soon.

"We just found out today. Don't worry, it's only for three weeks," he offers.

"Wow—no—that's cool." I struggle. "I mean, no, it's not cool because I'm not supposed to say that, but, um . . . are you gonna miss me?"

"Are you going to miss me?" He smiles.

"Totally," I say. "Do y'all get your own tour bus?"

"More like a crappy van." Oliver laughs.

"You didn't answer my question," I say.

"Of course I'm going to miss you. That's why I have to get an extra dose of you now," he answers.

With Weezer's *Pinkerton* on the stereo (the perfect make-out soundtrack), Oliver pulls me onto his lap, kissing me. His hands slide under my shirt, up to my shoulders and down to my lower back. He traces his fingers along the waist of my jeans, moving them beneath the elastic band of my underwear.

I move my hands under his threadbare T-shirt, feeling his tight shoulder blades. I drop my head, kissing that favorite freckle of mine on his shoulder.

With his hand gripping the back of my neck, Oliver pulls me back up to make my face meet his. He lightly brushes his mouth against mine before firmly biting / sucking my lower lip. I don't know what that move is called, but me-ow! My breathing immediately changes. And so does Oliver's.

He quickly pulls off my shirt, which I take as my cue to relieve him of his. His hands, now on a mission, slide down my jeans, roam over my thighs, and work their way up the inside of my leg. It feels, like—I dunno—terrifying and amazing at the same time. I raise my hips toward him, aching for him to touch me. . . .

But as soon as his fingers make their move, I jump, suddenly scared and distracted and aware of the party carrying on just outside the flimsy bedroom door, and

I don't want Oliver to hate me and storm out of the room. I just want to tell him I love him (do I? I think I do). And I want him to tell me he loves me. Does he?

Is it lame to want that?

He gives me a confused look. I exhale slowly, take his hand, and place it back on my thigh, giving him the go-ahead. I want it. Again, Oliver's fingers glide up my thigh and . . . again, I jump.

"Don't tell me you forgot to shave one of your legs again," Oliver whispers / smiles into my ear.

"No. I just . . ." I stammer.

"You're funny." He laughs.

"No, I'm not," I protest.

"Yes, you are. It's not like we're in high school, like we've never done this before, right?"

Um, yeah. Speak for yourself, pal.

I sit up and sigh apologetically. "I'm sorry. Just not here, okay?"

After several minutes of awkward silence, filled in ironically by Weezer's "Why Bother?" playing on the stereo—

> *Why bother*
> *It's gonna hurt me*
> *It's gonna kill when you desert me!*

Oliver says, "Let's go back to the party." He stands, holds out his arm, and pulls me off the floor.

Sleepover (& Under)

At the end of the party (which is a relative term because for a handful of girls, there's never an end to the party—they just keep going and going, the Energizer bunnies of good times), I follow Oliver out to his car.

He grabs me with his skinny, muscular, guitar-playing arms and says, "That's it. I'm kidnapping you. You're going home with me."

Considering Pash bailed on me, I decide to give in to his criminal ways. Though I warn him, "Just don't expect to get any good ransom money from my family."

"I'm not in it for the money." He smiles wickedly.

We drive to the house he shares with Hank, Eric, and Jesse (his two other bandmates). I'm not really sure what

I was expecting, but let me tell you, when four dudes live together, it is not pretty. Their place is a sty.

Not that I'm little miss merry maid, but clearly the boys are living in the dark ages of cleanliness. In their domestic world, little things like feather dusters and vacuums have yet to be invented.

I'm not saying it's not cool—it is. It's just . . . I'm afraid to sit.

Oliver looks at me, a little embarrassed. "Uh, yeah, the living room is kinda no-man's-land. I promise my room's not so scary," he says, tugging me by the hand toward the hallway.

"You're just trying to have your way with me," I say.

"Maybe," he says. "Maybe not."

We enter his bedroom, and I can confirm that, while it's muuuuch cleaner, it's still just messy enough for me to respect him. I plunk myself on the mattress that sits sans bed frame in the corner. (A look I tried to do in my own bedroom till Brooke put the kibosh on it. I told her it looked "cool and minimalist." She said it looked "homeless.")

"Sorry it's so tiny," Oliver says, "but I'm the youngest, so they gave me the smallest room. Bastards."

I think his room is perfect and a little mysterious, filled with all sorts of Oliver-centric, boy stuff. It's like a music lab with a bed. Lots of cables, guitar pedals, an amp with the screen torn off that he's repairing, a million

CDs, an old reel-to-reel tape recorder, and something he explains is a "four-track analog recorder because Pro Tools sounds too slick."

He has a Stooges poster and a picture of Joan Jett in her Runaway years, a stick of Right Guard deodorant sitting on an overturned milk-crate bedside table, and all his clothes are on the floor in his closet. One thing is hanging up—a blue, super-preppy, Banana Republic button-down with the tags still on it.

"Yeah, my mom got me that for my birthday." He laughs as he fishes through some records, then puts on Bob Dylan's classic *Highway 61 Revisited*. I can't argue with that.

We end up sitting on, then laying on his bed, fooling around, talking, listening to music, fooling around some more, listening to more music, talking about how tired we are, then fooling around again.

It feels so perfect just being next to him, I totally forget that in less than forty-eight hours he will be gone.

Now, do not ever repeat this to Pash, but I'm starting to think of Oliver as my best friend. Maybe I can have two best friends, one I make out with (O.), and one I make fun of people at school with (P.). I can tell Oliver anything, and I think he feels the same way.

For instance, we're laying there, and we start talking about having sex—and not in a completely embarrassing way. Just casual. Like, should we do it now? Or should we wait until he gets back from the tour? We weigh the pros and cons. I can tell he really wants to do it (I mean I can *feel* he does—*ahem*), but he sort of leaves it up to me.

Don't get me wrong, I'm up to the task (at least I think I am), but I want it to be right. And what's the rush? I guess it's kind of prudish, but I think maybe it might be better if we wait till he gets back from touring, give us something to look forward to.

So, around five A.M., with slivers of orange sun sneaking through his blinds, Oliver and I fall asleep tangled up together. No sex, just cuddling, which is so geeky, but the kind of geeky that feels heavenly.

Oh, It's Such a Perfect Day, I'm Glad I Spent It with You

When I stir the next morning, Oliver's already up. He's looking at me and smiling in this super-dopey, lovey way that's so not cool but it totally breaks my heart. I didn't know he had that cuteness in him. I want to bottle it and save it forever.

"What are you doing?" I say, sleepy-voiced, throwing my hands over my face.

"Just looking at you," he says, yawning. Man, if Malice saw Oliver this way, she would totally agree that he's not like all the other crummy band guys. She would change her tune—pun intended.

"Well, stop it," I say, burying my head in his chest.

"Fine," he says. "I'll never look at you again."

"Good. I don't want you to."

"Good, then I won't," he says as he kisses my cheek.

It's almost one in the afternoon, and technically I should get my ass home to Bodeen (oh, yeah, Bodeen), but I decide to push my luck a little bit further. When Oliver's in the bathroom, I call home and say that I'm still at Pash's, and we are working hard on our economics project that is due this week.

"Okay, honeybunch. Y'all don't work too hard," my mom says in a rare and surprisingly agreeable mood. I kind of wish she'd put up more of a fight because now I have a little acorn of guilt sitting in the bottom of my stomach. It's so much easier to defy her when I'm mad at her.

Of course, when I mentally reenter Oliver World (it used to be called Austin, but now, to me, it's Oliver World), the guilt subsides—mostly.

For his last day in town, I throw Oliver an on-the-move going away party for one, hitting all his favorite Austin spots: Hyde Park Pharmacy (for a few farewell rounds of Stampede), Tamale House, Waterloo Records, and Peter Pan Putt-Putt (home to a gigantic Peter Pan sculpture that was made in the '60s to be friendly and welcoming to kids but is actually creepy and terrifying—in short, awesome). Before we know it, evening is sneaking up on us.

"I seriously have to get back," I say, a little apologetically.

"No," Oliver says.

"Yes."

"Uh-uh, you can't leave me hanging my last night in town."

"You suck," I say, feeling tormented. Okay, someone tell me again why I can't just skip to being eighteen already and put this little issue of having to ask my parents' permission for everything behind me? It's not fair.

He relents, and as we head back for Bodeen, we pull over for gas. Oliver goes in to pay, and my heart says, *Noooooo! This day can't end! Not yet.* I grab Oliver's cell and call home again, really, really pushing my luck.

I make sure to dial our home digits, which rings to my mom's prized antique phone with the rotary dial. Brooke loves that phone for its old-fashioned charm, but I adore it for its genius lack of caller ID.

"Mom, can I please, please, please stay over at Pash's tonight?"

"It's a school night," my mom says.

"Exactly. We're doing schoolwork. We're gonna be up really late finishing our project, and we need to use her computer because ours is not as fast. There's no way we'll get it done," I lie. Our project isn't even really due until Wednesday (which reminds me, I need to get started on that collage).

There are several seconds of silence on the other end and then finally, "And that's okay with Pash's mom? This makes two nights in a row, Bliss."

"Of course, Mom. They're all about the grades over here. Pash is a very good influence."

"Fine, but this is a one-shot deal. Don't get used to it. You still live in my house," she says.

"I understand. Thank you! I love you!" I hang up just as Oliver opens the door and climbs back in the car. I greet him with a radiant grin.

"What?" he says.

"Turn around," I say. "I'm staying with you tonight."

The final night is pretty much a repeat of the previously perfect evening. We try to stay up as late as we can, so as not to sleep through our last hours together.

And then somewhere around 1:37 A.M., Oliver's in bed next to me, strumming his guitar, and I change my mind. I take the guitar out of his hands and . . . attack him, basically.

We "do the deed" as Pash would say, and not because he pushed or I wanted to be popular or because I have low self-esteem or anything girl-tragic like that, but simply because I want to. And, yes, we do use a condom, which Pash would be happy to know since she's always lecturing me about stuff like that, even though she's still a virgin.

Still, the first time totally hurts and ends with me practically yelling, "Get the hell off me."

Oliver gets really quiet. "Man. I feel like a dick."

"What for?" I ask.

"Because I didn't know it was your first time. Why didn't you tell me?"

"I dunno," I say. "I just didn't want it to be a 'thing,' you know?" I pull his arm around me. And we fall asleep in that position for a couple of hours before we wake up and start making out and fooling around and, well, we're at it again.

I don't know if it's the same for every girl, but for me, the second time is much better. And by the third, I decide this sex thing rocks—thank God. I was a little scared that I might hate sex.

We just had to figure out how to do it right.

167

Au Revoir

$\mathcal{T}$he next morning, when Oliver drops me off in front of the Gundersons' house, I start to regret the sex part. Not really, but I just feel so close to him, like I didn't even know it was possible to feel that close to another human being, and now I have to let him go for three loooong weeks.

I don't want to say good-bye. I want to have more sex.

I can tell Oliver feels the same by the way we both refuse to officially say good-bye. We sit in his car for an eternity avoiding those awful words and then we stand by his car even longer, still ignoring the reality of the situation.

It's one of those early, cold mornings, where fall is flirting with turning into winter. It's cold, and I huddle against Oliver, shivering.

The band van is leaving Austin at nine sharp, which Oliver says is Hank-speak for nine-thirty, but he has to get back to Austin because he hasn't even packed yet. I can understand. The boy's been a little distracted. And naturally, I have to be at school in twenty minutes.

We stand there, eking out every last second with each other, trying not to say it. He just rubs my hair as I lean into his chest.

There's a lot that I want to say.

I want to say I think all this emo stuff is retarded, and girlie-girls mooning over boys always seemed lame with a capital *L*. And I know I'm sarcastic and defensive and I make a joke out of everything and am highly resistant to anything that reeks of sentimental corniness, but I'm giving you my heart anyway because being with you feels like home, and I know you won't break it.

I want to tell him I love him. And mostly, I want to hear him say he loves me because I can feel it.

But maybe it's too soon for all of that, so I finally whisper, "Oliver."

"Yeah?"

"I want you to have something," I say, digging into my bag. I pull out my beloved Stryper T-shirt and hand it to him.

"No way," he says. "This is the coolest thing anyone's ever given me."

"Well, it is a guy's shirt. You can rock it," I say.

"I'll guard it with my life," he says, squeezing me tight. After a moment, he steps back. "Close your eyes."

I do. I hear fidgeting and feel something cover my shoulders, then I hear the zipper.

"Open 'em," Oliver says. I look down and realize I'm wrapped in his hoodie—his Stampede, high-score hoodie.

"I'll guard it with my life," I say.

We finally agree not to say good-bye. So, as Oliver's car pulls away, I shout, "Hello!"

"Howdy!" he shouts back, disappearing down the street. I have never hated the idea of three weeks more in my entire life.

# Feel Sorry for Me

*H*eading into school after my momentous weekend feels like three giant life steps backward. I've suddenly grown past this town, this quaint little high school thing. I wrap Oliver's hoodie around me for consolation.

I look up and see Pash camped out at my locker. Even from a distance, I can tell she's pissed. I don't know what for, but I'm sure I'm about to find out.

"Hey, Pash—" I start.

"Don't 'hey, Pash' me," she says, cutting me off.

"What? What'd I do?"

"You left me at the derby bout, you idiot. I had to go to the party all by myself, and when I got there they wouldn't let me in because too many people were already there. They were worried about another fire marshal bust."

"Pash! I didn't even know," I say.

"I sat outside for an hour waiting for you. Until I gave up and drove home."

"I'm sorry. I texted you. Why didn't you text me back?"

"You texted me?" she says, unconvinced. "Well, I didn't get it. Just tell me you have our damn collage."

"Collage?" I say. "What collage?"

"The collage. For our economics project," she says, overenunciating every word, as though English were my second language.

"Pash, calm down," I say. "I have two days to finish."

She stops and looks at me. "No you don't. It's due third period, as in today!"

"No it's not. It's due Wednesday," I argue, as if saying it out loud will make it so. The only thing it makes is Pash more pissed off. She spins back to me and lets it rip, talking a thousand miles a minute.

"Bliss! I did the whole report by myself, and all you had to do was the stupid, rinky-dink collage. Easy A for both of us, and you can't even do that. Y'know, not everyone has Roller-Derby-rock-star-boyfriend life to fall back on. If I can't make valedictorian at this joke of a school, I won't get a scholarship, which means I can probably kiss being a surgeon good-bye. I'm not just a grade whore, y'know. I'm trying to get out of this crappy town. Just like you."

"Pash," I say, feeling like a piece of mud on the bottom of a shoe. She waves me off with a dismissive flick of the wrist.

"Whatever. Thanks for never hanging out with me anymore. Thanks for standing me up at the party. Thanks for using me as a decoy so you can spend the night with your stupid boyfriend. But most of all, thanks for ruining my GPA. You're an awesome friend, Bliss," she says with brutal sarcasm. "Don't ever talk to me again."

Before I can respond to the conversational grenade, Pash turns and disappears into the hallway crowd. I feel like I'm gonna puke.

In third period, I plead with Mr. Smiley to punish me, not Pash, for the lack of collage action happening in our project. Yoda-man is not having it. I can feel Pash glaring at me from her seat in the back of the class. When I try to catch her eye, she defiantly turns her gaze in another direction.

I lost my best friend, and the truth is Pash is right. What kind of total lame-o flakes on an easy A when Pash is doing the heavy lifting? Me. I suck.

For the rest of the week, I try desperately to lure Pash back into the friendship fold, but she won't take the bait. I can't catch her at her locker, no matter how much I stake it out. Every time she sees me coming, she promptly turns and goes the other way. And during lunch, she disappears. (Is she eating in some dark corner of the library? I wonder.)

By Thursday, I start leaving hilarious notes in her locker (genius observations about the suckiness of Bodeen High, the kind of stuff she adores), but every one is boomeranged back to my locker with "return to sender" angrily scribbled in Pash's handwriting.

It hurts. I remember the days when that handwriting was used for me, not against me.

I know, I know. I fucked up. You don't have to rub it in.

This Is How I Roll

*I*n light of the great Pash Amini / Bliss Cavendar Best Friend Break-up of 2007 and Oliver touring, I'm back to riding the bingo shuttle to get to Austin. Not that I mind. It's cool to hang with Helen again. We blue-haired gals gotta stay together, especially in times of crisis.

I even keep my iPod tucked in my backpack and hold Helen's ball of yarn as she knits and tells me all about her life. She complains about her "arthritic hands," but, I'm telling ya, Helen works those needles like a rock star. And I know from experience. I made the fatal error of attempting to knit a scarf last Christmas. What started out as a hopeful ball of yarn came out looking like a disfigured pot holder that had been run over by a car a hundred times. And I don't even have arthritis.

Along the way, I secretly wonder if my being super nice to Helen will earn me some Karma cred toward getting Pash back. Like, somewhere in the universe, the people who control these things are watching and thinking, "We can't keep Bliss from her best friend for too long. She's obviously a good person. Her footwork may be all wrong, but her heart's in the right place."

Maybe I'm grasping at straws. I just miss Pash, and it's a little scary to know 101 apologies mean zip, nada, nothing.

Who Even Thought of Calendars, Anyway?

At derby practice, Razor and the team captains announce a change in the season schedule. Due to the fire marshal snafu, it has been decided that the unfinished game between the Hurl Scouts and the Holy Rollers will be replayed this Saturday. That means the remaining games are all pushed back a week, including our league championships, which will now take place on November 17, instead of November 10.

Now, I don't really keep track of my life by calendars. I'm too busy goin' with the flow to be ruled by a bunch of little organized boxes with numbers on a piece of paper. That's Brooke Territory, and I try to stay far away from it. In hindsight, perhaps that's not the wisest choice.

I get home from derby practice, starved for nourishment. I go to the kitchen, where my mom asks how my study group was. "Awesome," I say, making a beeline for the fridge. I open it, and reach for the gallon of milk, which turns out to be nearly empty, a little gift from the heavens. It's one of those rare moments when I can brazenly drink right out of the jug without incurring my mother's wrath. I throw my head back, close my eyes, and enjoy every last drop. *Ahhhhhhhhh.*

Then I open my eyes and find myself staring at the heavily detailed "Cavendar Calendar of Events" covering the refrigerator door. Shania's name is all over that thing, with little pink, glittery tiara stickers noting her various pageant comings and goings. I barely get a mention, save for the token "Bliss: dentist" on November 2.

Then, I clue in a little closer. There is one tiara marked in my honor, the day of the Miss Bluebonnet pageant, which happens to be on . . . November 17. Wait—November 17?

The derby championship game and the Miss Bluebonnet pageant are on the *same night*? I have to tell you, that is the most wicked punch line I've ever heard in my life.

In my English class, when we were studying *Hamlet* and *Macbeth,* Mrs. Weaver would go on and on about how all the great Shakespearean characters have one "fatal flaw," the stubborn human error that is the source of their dramatic undoing.

I never thought I had a fatal flaw. Until now. Clearly, my inability to remember dates has cost me my best friend and now this.

I am so fucked. I'm fucked with whipped cream, sprinkles, and a cherry on top.

Resistance Is Futile

After much thinking, scheming, plotting, and planning, I decide the best way to deal with my impending doom is to just . . . ignore it. Short of faking my own suicide or getting abducted by aliens (which might be fun—if you know any aliens, let them know I'm up for a field trip), there's no way out of the Miss Bluebonnet trap.

So I might as well enjoy all the derby action I can get in the meantime. No matter what happens at the championships, after Saturday, everyone will know the Hurl Scouts have the Holy Rollers' number. Throughout the week, I push myself harder in practice, knowing that the rematch might be my last chance to really prove myself. And my team.

At school, I spend my lunch period huddled in the library, going over my Oliver e-mail, or rather, *not* going over my Oliver e-mail. I send him stuff, but I don't hear back.

Not that I really expect him to pull over at any and all Internet cafés and send me hourly updates when he's in the middle of touring with the Benedicts (um, hello). The real obstacle is me and my lack of cell phone. That puts our relationship at a serious texting handicap. Oliver might as well be dating an Amish girl. Still. It would be nice to check my in-box and see some love. All I get lately are ads from Urban Outfitters, which are only depressing because I'm so broke.

Really, I'm Fine—I Swear

*O*n Saturday, Bird-man calls in a panic and talks me into working the Oink Joint lunch shift. Normally I would say no freakin' way, but I figure the busywork will give my nervous energy an outlet before the game.

When I clock in at ten-thirty, I notice a familiar time card next to mine—Pash's. This is the first time we have worked together in ages, although "together" is a relative term. We ignore each other the entire time. No funny Polaroid shenanigans, no sarcastic musical numbers, no synchronized eye rolls when customers annoy us. I'm telling you, best-friend Siberia is one cold place. If you ever get sent there, I highly suggest bringing a parka.

At one point, a couple of old ladies in full tourist regalia (fanny packs and comfort shoes) dare each other to order the Squealer sandwich, as if it's the most outrageous idea ever. They giggle conspiratorially like the best of friends. Okay, I admit, they're old, uncool, and burdened with that unfortunate wing flab grandma-types get under their arms (dear God, please let that never happen to me), but Maybelle and Jolene are *so freakin' adorable*. When they tell me all about how they've been best friends since they were fifteen years old, riding the same bus to Beeville High, I nearly run to the kitchen and cry my eyes out by the deep fryer. But I can't, because Pash is working, and I refuse to give her the satisfaction of seeing me weep at work.

Bird-man tries to ease the pain as I refill the napkin dispensers. "Don't be fooled," he says. "She really misses you too." I nod. *Thanks for trying, Bird-man, but really— this problem is bigger than you and all your manager skills.*

At least he lets me clock out fifteen minutes early. I have just enough time to get home, hose the stench of barbecue off my body, and get back to the Oink Joint, where Malice has so generously offered to pick me up.

I felt embarrassed asking for a ride, but Malice wouldn't hear of it. "Oh, shut up," she said. "Of course I'll come and pick your stranded ass up. If we don't have Babe Ruthless, we don't have a team." It's nice to know one person who doesn't hate me.

However, once I get home, I discover a little hitch in my evening plans.

I walk into my bedroom and make the most shocking discovery of my entire life. My room is clean. The bed is made.

And you can even see the floor!

Something is definitely up.

A little background on the whole room-cleaning agenda. Three years ago, when I was thirteen, my mom and I went to war over the state of cleanliness in my room before Earl was forced to negotiate a complicated cease-fire. We agreed that, as long as I didn't leave clutter around the house or hoard any crumb-laden dinner plates under my bed, my room was my space. All mine.

This truce has kept things cordial, more or less, for nearly three years. I even let things slide when my mom entered my sacred space with the ugly pink suit last month. Clearly, my politeness in that situation only empowered her to encroach on my privacy even further, which is never a good thing. Ever.

And today, the skate hit the fan.

The Poster Coaster

So, I'm feeling like the star of my very own *Twilight Zone*, standing in this pristine bedroom I don't recognize. This morning I left my messy nest only to return to find a *Better Homes and Gardens* fantasy. Not my fantasy, but my mom's.

I look at my closed closet door and feel my face get hot. I run over, throw open the door, and there before me is a row of immaculately hung clothes.

I fall to my knees and dig to the waaaaay back of my closet, my secret hiding space for my derby gear—my skates, my helmet. I move my hand around, but all I feel is carpet.

"Where are my skates?" I ask myself out loud,

thinking, hoping, praying, maybe, just maybe, I put them somewhere else.

And then I feel it—her presence. Like Bigfoot's shadow descending over a helpless little bug in the forest. I turn and see my mother standing over me. And she does not look happy (that makes two of us).

"I have your skates," she says.

Ohhhhhhh. Fuuuuuuuck. What did she just say?

For a moment, I stare at her blankly, trying to figure out just how much she knows, so I know how to respond. Like, am I 50 percent in trouble? Or the whole 100 percent? And then I notice the rolled-up derby poster in her hand. *Okay, my life is over.*

"How long, Bliss?" she inquires, calmly. "How long have you been sneaking off behind my back and doing this . . . this Roller Derby thing?"

And immediately I get defensive. I mean, of course I know I'm going down, but not without a fight. And maybe fight's the wrong word. Honestly, I want her to understand that Roller Derby is really important to me, not something I chose just to piss her off.

"Mom, I know it looks really bad," I start, "but I can explain it."

"Bliss, I can't trust anything you say right now," she declares, turning and walking off, as if she is so betrayed that the mere idea of having a full conversation is too much for her.

But I'm not done. I have a game to skate tonight, and my ride is picking me up in thirty minutes. I need my gear. I need my skates, and I need to get the hell out of here. So I follow her into the living room, determined to negotiate the return of what is rightfully mine.

"Mom, we don't have to talk about this right now. Just give me my skates," I say in my most mature, let's-be-adults-about-this voice.

"That's not happening, Bliss," she counters, coldly.

"Give. Me. My. Skates," I say slowly, my last attempt at peaceful persuasion.

Brooke turns, looks me square in the eye, and says, "No." And that's when I start to crack.

"I paid for them! They're mine!" I spit out, to which she replies, "You're grounded until further notice," before shutting her bedroom door, which totally sends me over the edge.

I'm suddenly thinking how, year after year, I sucked it up and submitted myself to her parade of pageant humiliation, and she can't even *try* to understand how I might need a little part of my life for myself. It's not a topic of discussion because Brooke doesn't care, and if Brooke doesn't care, then it doesn't exist. I don't exist.

Well, too late, lady, you made me. I'm here, and I EXIST. So, deal!

Forget keeping the peace, forget staying out of trouble, forget trying to delicately sway her into giving me my skates back. I walk up to her bedroom door, throw it open, and practically scream, "You don't even know me!"

And, I swear to God, it takes every last ounce of self-control to keep me from following that sentence with "you fat bitch." But I keep that part internal, as I do not want to die immediately. Or regret being so harsh.

She looks at me and laughs—*she laughs!*—"Bliss, you're only sixteen. You don't even know who you are."

"I know I'm not Miss Bluebonnet," I say, throwing it back at her. "I know that much." I'm shaking. I feel like I'm on the verge of either crying my eyes out or kicking someone's ass—I just don't know which. But I know, even in my rage, punching my mom is not really an option.

My dad, hearing the commotion, comes running in from doing yard work outside. The minute poor Earl sees my mom and me dug deep in our mother / daughter World War III trenches, I can tell he'd rather be mowing the grass. Whatever is going on here, Earl wants nothing to do with it.

But it's too late. Mom is determined to get an ally and some extra muscle on her side. She waves the poster at him, like a betrayed woman in a Spanish soap opera. "This! This is what our daughter's been doing!"

Earl, probably still a little unsure what exactly it is my mom is having a meltdown about, takes a moment to digest the contents of the poster. And this is what happens. A grin actually spreads across his face, a little flicker of joy I will never forget till the day I die, and he says, "Roller Derby's back? Well, hell, we used to watch that on late-night TV. We'd get a case of Lone Star, go to Freddy Jasper's house, and have a—"

"Earl!" Brooke shouts, rocketing off the bed. "She's been doing it in secret behind our backs!"

Earl's smile immediately drops as he steps in line behind the Brooke regime. It makes me so sad that the tears I've been bravely fighting off start to sting my eyes and blur my vision.

"Please," I plead, like a prisoner begging to see the sun. "Just listen, okay? For the first time, I don't feel like a total freak or like something's wrong with me."

"You are not running around with those girls and their tattoos. It's not ladylike."

"Well, I guess we have different ideas about what it means to be a lady." I sigh. "I know I lied, and I'm really sorry. You can ground me later. But just let me go now. Please. Dad?"

My dad looks at me. I know he wants to say yes, but Brooke throws him an "Earl Cavendar, don't you even think about it" look, so he says, "You lied, kiddo. That dog ain't gonna hunt."

So I play the one card I have left. I turn, run to my room, and slam the door. Actually, I slam it twice just to really drive home the message: *I hate you both!*

Runaways—Joan Jett's First Band and Me

So, I'm sitting here in my made-over bedroom, picturing it catching on fire, which is a comforting thought, but only for a few minutes. I start to feel like I'm gonna jump out of my skin all over again.

This grounded-until-further-notice thing is total bullshit. My clock reads 5:13. Malice will be swinging into the OJ parking lot in seventeen minutes, and you know what? I'm going to be there to meet her. Skates or no skates, my ass will be in that seat and headed for Austin.

I grab my Emily-the-Strange satchel and stuff as many clothes as I possibly can in it, until the stitches are screaming and begging for mercy. Then I climb out the window and make a run for it.

I break into a dead sprint to meet Malice, which

sounds dramatic, but trust me, it's hard not to feel like a loser running through the streets of Bodeen, Texas, with an overstuffed Emily-the-Strange satchel slapping at your thigh and sliding off your shoulder every other step. But then again, I guess there's no cool way to spontaneously run away from home.

Thank God Malice is on time. She skids into the parking lot like a getaway car in a heist movie, complete with a fierce soundtrack blaring through her speakers: Thank you, New York Dolls. I throw open the passenger door and briefly look through the OJ window, where Pash and Bird-man are both working doubles (that's overachievers for ya). Bird-man mouths "good luck," while Pash scowls and turns away.

Backatcha, babe, I think as I slam myself into the safety and comfort of Malice's ride.

"Where's your gear, Ruthless?" Malice asks.

"Stolen," I answer, which is not entirely untrue.

"Shit. Well, don't worry. We'll get one of the girls to hook you up," she declares. She's a good egg, that Malice. Nothing's ever a problem. There's always a solution.

"Thanks," I say.

"Ready to kick some Holy Roller ass?"

"Malice, I've never been so ready in my entire life."

She gives a hell-yeah nod and holds up her hand. I slap it, thinking, *Bring it on, Dinah. I ain't afraid of you!*

I've got a lot of anger I need to work out tonight.

Age Discrimination

*U*pon our arrival, Malice heaves open the door to the Dollhouse.

"All right, bitches! One of you better lend Ruthless your size nines!" She shouts, to drown out the pregame activity—hammers getting busy on last-minute track repairs, girls discussing which eye shadow makes them look more badass—you know, the usual.

Only this time we are met by silence, and not a good silence. The kind of silence that slaps you in the face.

We see Razor huddling with the other team captains, and they all turn their heads as we walk in the door.

"What the fuck, y'all? Who died?" Malice asks, trying to shake them out of whatever it is they are so collectively tweaked about.

"Malice, we need to talk," Blade says. "Bliss, don't go anywhere."

Dinah gives me a smug look, and I still don't register the gravity of the situation. Sometimes I'm slow, but a few minutes later I am up to speed. Brace yourself—this isn't good.

Apparently it has come to the league's attention that I may not actually be eighteen, that I am, in fact, sixteen years old. Which, if you ask me, should be no big deal at this point. I can skate just as well as—or better than, some would say (not me, because I'm not conceited that way)—all the other girls. And Lord knows I can hold my own on the party front; no maturity gaps there. But there's just no pleasing some people.

In light of the fire marshal scandal the team captains are afraid of any issue that might jeopardize the league in any way, or, as Malice explains, "Ruthless, if you got hurt, your parents could sue us and shut us down entirely."

She sort of has a point. As annoying as my mother is, I could totally see her threatening a lawsuit. It would not be the first time. But I'm not about to admit that. I'm still hung up on why they are suddenly suspicious. I'm suspicious of their suspicions.

"Someone heard a cop say you were sixteen at the fire marshal bust," Juana says.

"Anonymous tip," Dinah adds, with so much pride

she might as well have I RATTED YOU OUT tattooed on her forehead. I knew she was low; I just didn't know she was this low.

If I weren't such a lady and a model citizen, I'd kick her in the face with my skate. If I had my skate. She's lucky I don't—let's just leave it at that.

Malice looks like she might cry when she says, "I'm sorry, Ruthless, but if you can't prove that you're eighteen, we can't let you play the game." Note to self: It's always good to have a fake ID. Just in case.

By this point, my entire team has gathered around us. I expect them to be pissed, to swarm me like a vicious girl gang on a point-proving mission and beat me to a pulp. Instead, they're all really kind and really . . . disappointed.

Finally, Emma says, "What if we get permission from your parents? If they agree to let you skate, we won't be liable." All the other girls pipe in with "yeah," "why not?" and "you should try that."

Really. They're sweet girls, but they have no idea what they're up against. I haven't even mentioned the fact that I ran away from home two hours ago.

They all turn and look at me, their hopes and dreams of this game sitting perilously on my skinny shoulders. And yet, their belief in me is seductive. I start to believe it too. And that kind of power can make you think things, do things—crazy things.

. . . In a Blaze of Glory

Riiing . . . riiing . . .

On a cell phone borrowed from Malice, I wait for my dad to pick up on the other end.

"Hello?"

"Um, Dad—"

"Bliss! Where on God's green earth did you disappear to? Your mama's beside herself. Are you safe?"

"Of course I'm safe."

"You sure?"

"No, Dad, I got kidnapped by a band of swarthy oil-men, and I'm on my way to Dubai to be wife number eight in a white-slavery harem."

"Is that your idea of humor?"

"Sort of. I'm fine, okay? I just have a quick question to ask you. Between you and me, Dad."

"When are you coming home?"

"Dad, I know you think my playing Roller Derby is kind of cool. You would never say so, but you're just as sick of the pageant dictatorship as me."

Silence.

"So, Dad, will you please give your word that you will not sue the Derby Girls if I skate? Mom doesn't have to know."

"Bliss."

"Please?"

An eternity of silence.

"Bliss, I'm gonna tell you somethin'."

"What?"

"I got two more years with you in my house. But I got a whole lifetime with your mama. You follow?"

"Yeah, I follow. You're never gonna stand up to her, are you?"

I don't know what I was thinking even calling him in the first place. I close Malice's cell and turn back to face my teammates' expectant faces.

"Sorry, y'all," I say, shaking my head.

"You tried," Crystal Deth says, adjusting her fishnets.

"You okay?" Malice asks.

"Yeah." I sigh. "But I kinda, sorta need to move in with you."

"Sure." She nods as she puts her arm around me.

And the Point of Even Playing Is . . . ?

I would love to infuse this part of the story with some kind of noble, "we did the best we could, we're still winners even though we lost—*boo-ya!*" spirit, but the simple truth is the Hurl Scouts got slaughtered by the Holy Rollers.

And of course Dinah is gloating all over the place like she's God's gift to derby, and I still want to kick her in the face with the skate I don't have, but I'm kind of busy at the moment. I'm on the phone.

As Malice's new official roommate, I now have access to a cell phone! So, I immediately dial Oliver, hoping to catch him before they go on in—where was it again?— Cleveland or Cincinnati? Not that it matters. What matters is that I need to hear his voice in the worst way.

Seriously. If Oliver can't be here to wrap his arms around me, then I'll happily wrap myself in the sound of his voice.

But all I get is voice mail. "Hey, it's Oliver. Leave me some love." *Beeeeep.*

Even though all I get is recorded-voice Oliver, it's comforting to hear actual evidence of his existence. I even skip leaving a message so I can redial and listen to his voice again . . . and maybe get him to answer. No dice. It goes to voice mail.

I take a deep breath and launch into a rambling message that, to the best of my memory, goes something like

this: "Hey, rock star, it's me. How's tricks? I'm okay, I guess. . . . Well, not really. I'm kind of at war with the world today, and the world is winning. Anyway, I sort of left home—long story—but you can call me back on Malice's phone. When you have time. . . . I miss your voice, and um . . . everything else."

Even though I'm pretty crestfallen at the moment (and believe me, whatever my crest is, it has fallen), I'm grateful to still have Oliver's hoodie. It's my new security blanket.

As I crash on Malice's futon (in Malice's perfect little apartment full of thrift-store fabulousness), I hear echoes of her playing the Velvet Underground in her room.

All I can think about is Oliver and how missing him

has suddenly gone from an annoyance to an ache. It physically hurts, from my stomach to the rest of my body.

I can't wait for him to call me back tomorrow so we can at least have a few minutes to talk.

My Illegal Guardian

Malice takes my moving in pretty seriously. She refuses to let me ditch school and insists on hauling her ass out of bed at "this fucking ungodly hour" to drive me back to Bodeen so that I won't miss my first class. She even makes me a sack lunch, which consists of a frozen burrito microwaved until hot, then stuffed in some foil to keep warm until lunchtime rolls around. And a past-its-prime banana to wash it all down. I guess it's the thought that counts.

Dropping me off at school, Malice sports a '60s psychedelic robe that is fashion's answer to coffee. One look at that Day-Glo garment and you are awake: Caffeine is no longer necessary. The robe elicits many a disapproving stare from my peers, but Malice gives just as good as she gets.

"Hey, shorty," she shouts out the window as Matt Holtzman passes and grimaces, "I wouldn't be caught dead in those pleated chinos, so suck it."

She turns to me and smiles. "Y'know, Bliss, if I had to endure this cultural wasteland on a daily basis, I would have run away and started playing Roller Derby too."

Finally. *Finally, someone who understands where I'm coming from.*

"Malice, will you adopt me?" I ask.

"No way. I can barely afford my own college tuition," she answers. And then she starts to get serious, like, school-counselor serious (only without the bad bumble-bee jewelry).

"Ruthless," she says, picking through a bag of questionably fresh Cheetos she just retrieved from under her car seat, "I love you to bits, we all do, but at some point, you're gonna have to go home and work things out with the 'rents."

"There's no way. They don't understand me."

"You have to give them the chance. My parents still think I'm a total freakshow, but I know they love me," Malice says. Her parents may have a point: She's wearing a flower-power robe, snacking on a bag of stale Cheetos, and sipping cold coffee from a "World's Greatest Grandpa" mug. Not every family would understand the Tao of the Malice.

"I'm all for raisin' hell," she adds, "but sometimes you gotta know when to make peace."

It's too early for me to digest this impromptu lecture, so I get out of the car and smile. "Thanks, Mom."

"'Bye, darling," she calls after me in her best 1950s June Cleaver voice. "Have a swell day at school!"

Without looking back, I flip her off and keep walking toward the door. I hear her honk in appreciation.

How could I ever go home to my fam now that I have Malice?

The Gift That Keeps on Giving

For losers like me, the only refuge is the school library. I'd love to say I've been devouring great literary works and constantly expanding my mind, but lately I've spent much of my time camped out on one of twenty-three computers, the central hub of Bodeen wi-fi.

Technically, we're only supposed to use the school computers for "work" (as several taped-up signs constantly remind us), but who are we kidding? It's a MySpace world, and I'm just living in it.

The best signs, though, are the neon yellow ones that gravely warn about venturing onto any "adult Web sites," aka downloading porn. Any student caught engaging in such inappropriate use of school property will be immediately expelled.

Despite the sinister warning, every year someone busts through the laughable security measures and starts a nipple free-for-all. While I admit high school boys drooling over pictures of tits and disgusting beaver shots falls into the category of "totally lame," there's something even lamer about adults so clueless they can't figure it out. Plus, it's funny, and I root for funny every time.

Personally, I'm grateful for the free computer access. My loser lunch period goes by much faster when I can take my mind off the fact that I have no real friends and cruise around MySpace with my fake ones. Although, I must confess, I may be outgrowing that addiction.

I check in on the Stats' Web site, curious to see if Dylan, their drummer and nerd extraordinaire, has posted any updates. Nothing.

I wonder if Oliver is calling me on Malice's phone right now. Ugh. Malice should have let me skip school just so I could be there when Oliver calls back.

I move on to the Tour Scrapbook, which is a new addition to the site. *Ooh. So that's where Dylan's been posting the new goodies.* I scroll through the tour pics, all of which fall into one of three categories: (1) someone in the band playing onstage, usually bathed in blue light, occasionally red; (2) the band at some crummy restaurant eating cheap food; and (3) members of the band, sweaty from having just played a set, holding a bottle of beer in one hand and a cigarette in the other while chatting with some random person they've clearly just met. Fans.

I don't know how to explain it, but seeing pictures of Oliver makes me feel homesick for him. I didn't know you could be homesick for a person, especially when they're the one traveling. But I am. I guess Oliver is where my heart lives.

I glance at the printers near the library check-out desk, trying to gauge whether or not I can get away with covertly copying my favorite Oliver picture. I nearly die when I see it. He's playing bass in classic Oliver head-down, hair-in-the-face mode, but you can see one of his eyes peeking out from under his mop, and he has a little smile. Like he's trying to be cool, but he's having so much fun he can't help himself. And best of all, Oliver's wearing my beloved Stryper shirt. Onstage!

I never thought a picture of '80s metalheads in spandex pants could look so sexy, but when that image is stretched over the broad shoulders and chest of my boy on bass—swoonalicious.

But then, like some criminal act that changes your life forever, something goes wrong. Terribly wrong.

I notice another picture of my Stryper shirt. I can't quite make out what's going on in that small frame, but—

My heart races as I click on the thumbnail. The picture suddenly fills my screen with a brutal truth I'm not at all prepared for, as if I was skipping down the street on a sunny day and then—*whammo*—from nowhere, I got hit by a car.

My Stryper shirt is definitely in the picture, and so is Oliver, but he's not wearing said Stryper shirt. Someone else is. A girl, a blond, smiling girl who I'd like to now and forever refer to as That Fucking Whore in My Stryper Shirt. And she is all over Oliver. Not just her hands and body but traces of her lipstick. And they look disgustingly happy.

Apparently Oliver had quite the good time with TFWIMSS. After a little more detective work, I see them in the background of a Hank picture, making out against the van.

Now that I think of it, getting hit by a car would have been better than this. At least I'd be unconscious by now.

Instead, I'm awake, wide awake. My entire body feels like it's on fire, and I have to get the hell out of here. Away from this computer, this library, this school, this town, this planet.

I have to go.

Run Forest Run

*S*tudies show that people in crises can achieve amazing feats of physical strength, which probably explains how I manage to sprint right past the school security guard and out the front door. Bodeen High supposedly has a zero-tolerance policy on things like a girl running out the front door in the middle of the school day, but a girl with a freshly broken heart blowing past security? They don't stand a chance.

All I know is I have no idea where I'm going and I can't stop running. I feel so raw the sun hurts, the breeze stings, and I can't get away from this tidal wave of sudden pain that has me pinned against the shore.

What the fuck just happened?

My mind races with a highlight reel of all things Oliver—seeing him at the first derby bout when he was just Señor Smolder, listening to the Velvet Underground with him, the surprise of him standing in the Oink Joint parking lot, playing Stampede, talking at three A.M., kissing him, getting kissed by him, music, music, music, and laughing, laughing, laughing.

It was all a lie.

What did I do wrong? Why wasn't I good enough? And how could Malice be right?

I tried to be cautious, I tried to keep him at bay with sarcasm and innocent hang-outs to prove I wasn't easy, to prove that I wasn't going to fall all over myself just to be with a boy who plays guitar. I made him prove himself to me, I made him earn it—and he did. And then I gave it up to him: my trust, my heart, my soul, everything. I gave it up to him five times in his bedroom while I completely forgot about my best friend.

And now . . . I just wish I could get it back.

208

Low, Lower, Lowest

I must've blacked out because I don't know who or what brought me here. All I know is I'm sitting on the floor of a familiar-looking kitchen in front of a giant refrigerator door.

It occurs to me that I'm hungry. Well, not so much hungry as desperately feeling the urge to shove as much food as I can into my mouth to keep from screaming. Make sense? Of course not, but I'm in a painful free fall.

I yank open the fridge and start emptying its contents onto the floor around me until I strike gold with a Tupperware of leftover shepherd's pie. I heart shepherd's pie. I peel back the Saran Wrap cover and go to town.

I hear the faint jingling of keys in the distance but continue eating, trying to distract myself from all the hopeful "this must be some misunderstanding—Oliver really loves me" thoughts coming out of my mind.

It's hard to lie to yourself if you're a smart person, even when you feel stupid. Half-assed, needy explanations aren't going to change what I now know about Oliver. I feel so . . . used.

I look up, and there she is—Brooke. I'm so loony right now, I didn't even realize I was in my own house. That was not the plan. (Okay, there wasn't a plan, per se, but I didn't expect to end up here.)

She looks at me. I look at her.

I haven't been home in three days, but it feels like three years. She can't begin to imagine what I've been through. Like a cornered and confused animal, I start to panic, wanting to escape but unsure how.

I can't even find my words. All I can say is "please, just—" before the Hoover Dam holding back my tears starts to crumble and out spills the tidal wave. I'm sure it gives her triumphant satisfaction to see me weeping uncontrollably in front of a tub of shepherd's pie, but I can't stop.

Brooke takes one step toward me, and I brace myself for whatever new round of fighting she's about to suck me into. I don't care if I'm grounded till I'm sixty-five, I just don't have the energy right now. Whatever it is, she wins.

But something else happens. She throws her hand over her heart and sighs, "Oh, honeybunch . . ."

She kicks a tub of fake butter out of the way and kneels beside me. I'm crying so hard, it takes me several seconds to realize my mom's arms are around me, rocking. She's warm and soft and it feels so good, like I'm five years old and she's scooping me up with her love.

You can laugh, but that's the truth.

Maybe it's some secret unspoken mother/daughter language, but even though I've never uttered a peep to her about Oliver, she seems to *just know* why I'm so devastated. She brushes my hair back and says only one thing. "Whoever he is, he doesn't deserve you."

"Mom, I think I'm gonna die," I say.

"No, you're not."

"No, really, I think I am. He gave her my Stryper shirt, and she was wearing it. How do you do that to someone?"

My mom just keeps hugging me, then says, "Stryper? I saw them when I was a freshman at Texas Christian. Good Lord, those boys had bigger hair than I did."

I laugh. The idea of my mother rocking out to '80s Christian heavy metal—singing along to "To Hell with the Devil"—is so accidentally cool. She has no idea.

Cupcake

*O*kay, say it. Go ahead. I got my heart broken by _____ (I don't say his name anymore), and the first thing I do is run home to my mommy. Well, so what? I don't care if I'm uncool. I'm just trying to survive at this point. My heart's on life support.

I get to my room and nap for about a thousand years, total sleep coma. As cool as being Malice's temporary roommate is, I can't get a good night's sleep over there. This stupid room, in this stupid house, in this stupid town is where I sleep best. I guess it's home. For now.

I wake up to one of my favorite smells, warm cupcakes. Mom knocks on my door and enters carrying a plate of fresh-baked (from scratch) chocolate cupcakes, with chocolate filling and chocolate frosting. They are a total sugar bomb, but soooo good on the rare occasion.

"Thanks, Mom, but I'm not really hungry," I say.

She sets the plate down by my stereo. "In case you change your mind."

I immediately do and reach for a cupcake.

My dad wanders in from the hall. "There you are." He smiles. "You're lucky you showed up. I was about to colonize your room myself. Turn it into a football-watchin' room. Get me a flat screen and—"

I give him a "don't you dare think about painting little footballs on bedroom walls" look, and he slugs me in the arm.

"Good to see ya back, kiddo."

"Yeah, sorry I was such a bitch to you on the phone."

Dad waves his hand like it was nothing. "Already forgotten." He kisses my forehead, swipes one of my cupcakes, and leaves.

As my mom exits my room, she adds, "I think we can forget the grounding thing for now, don't you?"

So, I guess the secret recipe for getting your parents to be cool is have a big fight, then run away, and return three days later an emotional train wreck. They can't come down on you then. Which is nice. I don't know if I could take it right now.

Getting my heart stomped by ＿＿＿ is already punishment enough.

In light of such parental coolness, I decide to meet my mom halfway.

"Mom. If you really want me to be in the Miss Blue-bonnet pageant, I will," I say. She turns back.

"Well, I wouldn't want to push you."

"No. I want to do it," I say, which is kind of a lie, but it's not like it's going to kill me. One last pageant hoorah. I'll go out with a bang.

My mom perks up. "Well. That would do my heart good."

Pash Part 2

I figure if my mom and I can find some common ground, then there's hope for me and Pash.

I get up early, dash over to her house, and sneak into the backseat of her car, lying in wait. She doesn't even notice me when she chucks her books in the backseat as she gets ready to leave for school. The books barely miss making contact with my face. It is by the grace of her sloppy throwing skills that I still have my nose.

Pash starts the car and cranks up the Killers' new CD (*What? I thought we agreed, except for the seductive charms of "Mr. Brightside," that band was all hype.*)

I let her cruise a few blocks before I rise out of the backseat like a creature from a slasher flick. Pash screams and slams on the brakes.

"Dammit, Bliss. You scared the shit out of me!" she yells into her rearview.

"Sorry," I offer. "I just had to talk where you couldn't walk off or hang up. Plus, you never lock your doors, so consider this a lesson. What if I were some creepy guy? You would be so kidnapped right now.".

Pash rolls her eyes. "Just spit it out."

"Look, I know I've been exiled from the Queendom of Pash and I totally deserve it. I've been a crappy friend, and no matter what happens, I just want you to know how sorry I am that I screwed up your GPA. That's all."

Pash slows at a stoplight, and I shimmy from the backseat to the front, opening the door to let myself out. At the last second, I feel a hand grip the back of my cardigan.

"Get back in here, you dork," Pash says. And just like that, she reopens the pearly gates of her friendship.

"I missed you!" I beam as we hug.

"Missed you too. You're lucky I'm still first in our class, or this would not have worked out."

As much as best-friend purgatory blows, it feels so good to be forgiven that screwing up was almost worth it. Almost.

A Week Later

𝒫ash and I fall back into synchronized best-friend step, which provides much relief from my Miss Bluebonnet preparation. Nothing takes your mind off promenading down a long stage in a frock covered with appliqué blue-bonnets like stealing tube socks from Wal-Mart. All of it helps keep my mind off _____ and his lying ways. It hurts if I think about it too long, and I don't want to give him that power over me. He doesn't deserve it.

Pash even backs me up with a little ex-boyfriend therapy. We burn _____'s hoodie in a field by the Oink Joint, along with every mixed CD he ever gave me. It's harsh, but so was he—it had to be done. Otherwise, I'd be too tempted to obsess over him.

At work, Pash remains skeptical of my plans to

participate in Miss Bluebonnet. "You're selling out," she says when I clock in, fresh from the Curl Up & Dye Hair Salon, sans blue hair.

But Pash doesn't understand. She wasn't there when my mom picked my mess of a self off the kitchen floor without a single criticism. Plus, this one pageant is a tradition with the Cavendar girls. My g-ma scored that crown, and so did my mom; I should at least try. Not that I expect to win. Let's get real. Come Saturday, it's going to be the Corbi show from start to finish.

And don't worry. The minute the crown's awarded, I'm going back to my Manic Panic blue.

There's another nugget of info from the Great Bliss Cavendar / Pash Amini Best-Friend Reconciliation that I must share. Hold on to your hats, kids, this one is a real doozie.

Pash and Bird-man are officially an item. Sort of. You heard me. My bombshell BFF and our stick-figure Oink Joint manager have coupled up.

I really have no way of explaining this shocking turn of romantic events, so without further ado, I give you Pash Amini in her own words:

Bliss, I was in a bad place, okay? You abandoned me, I was, like, two inches off the ground depressed, and my "Pash Amini Best iPod Mix Ever" project was going nowhere. It was Saturday night,

*and Bird-man was lecturing me about how to
clean the grill, and I dunno, I just grabbed him. I
wanted to hit him, but somehow I ended up kissing him. There's no excuse, but I did it. Of course, I
immediately shoved him away and said, "Get over
it. That will never happen again."*

*But the thing is—and here's where it gets
weird—Bird-man is an amazing kisser. It's like he's
got lightning bolts for lips. I kept thinking about it.
I had to go back for more. And I also couldn't help
thinking about what good friends we had become
since I wasn't hanging out with you.*

*At first it was just a desperation thing, but you
know what? Once Bird-man gets over that trying-
too-hard-to-be-cool thing, he really is . . . cool. He's
smart, he's funny, knows all sorts of fun useless infor-
mation, and he has an open mind about good music.*

*Of course, he's hopeless on the fashion front, but
I'm working on that. Did you notice, he shaved his
starter mustache? Yeah, you can thank me for that.*

God, he's a good kisser.

Then Pash flops on my bed with a dreamy sigh.

"You're not going to make him get a Mohawk, are
you? Because I don't think the world is ready for a half-
bald Bird-man," I say, trying to adjust to the weirdness of
Pash and him as a couple.

"Never!" she promises.

"Well, then. I'm really happy for you."

She bolts up, all defensive and sharp. "Don't be yet. Bird-man's *not* my boyfriend. He's just a . . . development." Yeah, right. Something tells me Pash and Mr. Lightning Bolts for Lips will be an official item sooner than later.

And honestly. There's no denying Bird-man's well-intentioned heart. He's a good guy, not the type of prick who would take your favorite Stryper T-shirt on tour and bequeath it to some random trollop he hooks up with while conveniently forgetting you ever existed.

As Pash is schooling me in the finer points of all things Bird-man, my dad knocks on the door. "Bliss, telephone. Someone named Malice? In Wonderland?" He asks like he's unsure if I would really know someone with such a name.

"Thanks, Dad. I got it," I say, reaching for the phone.

"Hey, Malice, what's up?" I can hear the sounds of a four-alarm derby fiesta in the background. The Hurl Scouts are busy getting ready for next Saturday's championship game, a rematch against the Holy Rollers that will be pretty pointless.

"Ruthless!" Malice shouts. "Please tell me you're at least coming to the bout to cheer us on." I can hear Kid Vicious, Crystal Deth, and Emma Gedden crowd around Malice's phone.

"Yeah," Crystal yells, "you're the soul of our team."

"I can't. That's the same night as my pageant. I'll be there in spirit," I offer. As if that ever means anything.

When I hang up the phone, Pash looks at me. "You miss it, don't you?"

"Nah."

"You're the worst liar ever," she says before steering the conversation back to her and Bird-man, because we really haven't discussed it enough tonight. *ZZZZzzzzzzzzzzzzzz.*

Sash Rash

*H*oly moly, if I thought my mother's tiara affliction was something to cringe at before, that was only a warm-up for who she becomes the day of Miss Bluebonnet. Ladies and gentlemen, behold: Pageant-zilla.

Every hour on the hour, I'm getting prepped, plucked, and prodded, and we're not even at the country club yet.

Does she think I can really win? I want to raise my hand midway through the day and say, "Hello, remember me? I'm Bliss, I'm the one who gets the 'Certificate of Participation,' not the crown." Not that it would stop her. She's a woman on a mission, and this is my last-ever pageant, so what's to rebel against? (Okay, yes, there is *much* to rebel against anytime girls are being rewarded for their beauty with a sparkly crown, but this is the new me, the mature me, the me that is trying to keep the peace.)

Two hours, one custom-made gown, and a hundred pictures later, I am parked backstage at my own mirror, doing my makeup. I've brought Pash with me to be my good-luck charm, but really it's just to keep me company so I don't go insane and start killing all the other annoying pageant girls.

As Corbi and all the Corbi wannabes run around backstage in an unspoken competition for who can be the most dramatic, Pash and I chill at my mirror. When I start applying the blue eye shadow, Pash starts pretending to go into convulsions.

"Stop it," I say, laughing, making the application of my hideous makeup even worse.

"I can't watch you do that to your face," she declares.

"Hey," I argue, "if I win, we get free Bluebonnet ice cream for a year."

"Then spackle that glitter on!" she barks, flipping through someone's abandoned copy of US Weekly. She makes fun of all the overhyped, underfed actresses. "I think you should donate your ice cream to these girls."

"Yes," I say. "For all the starving girls in Hollywood, this rocky road's for you!"

This adventure would not be nearly as fun without the Pash Amini Show. Even my mom leaves me in Pash's capable hands and buzzes around the audience, working the room as she likes to do in Pageantville.

At around 6:07, we are given notice that the show will start promptly at 6:30 and we should be ready in our "daytime formal" wear, which is a long-winded way of saying "suit."

At 6:11, the backstage emergency exit door flies open, and in walks the craziest culture clash the Bodeen pageant world has ever seen.

All I hear is Emma Gedden's voice say, "Drop the pink lip gloss and step away from the mirror." I turn to see my entire Roller Derby team—every single one of the Hurl Scouts—strutting through the backstage area.

Crystal looks just as shocked to see me as I am to see her. "Ruthless, what happened to your hair? I've seen parade floats smaller than that."

"Well," I say, patting my teased and sprayed updo, "This is how we roll in Bodeen."

"Exactly why we have to get you out of here," Kid Vicious declares.

"What?" I ask, slowly wrapping my head around the surreal fact that my derby life and my pageant life are colliding in front of my very eyes.

"We took a poll," Crystal says in between throwing a couple of hilarious I-will-fuck-you-up stares at Corbi, "and the Scouts decided we'd rather forfeit the championships than skate without Babe Ruthless."

"I say you run," says Pash, throwing her support to their cause.

"You freaks!" I say, completely flattered. "It rules that you came here. But there's no way I can flee without killing my mom."

And as if on cue, I hear her wandering through the dressing room.

"Bliss . . . ? Bliss Cavendar, where are you?" she calls.

I turn white, whiter than normal—translucent.

"Y'all, my mom's coming. Hide!" I say, flailing my arms in full spazz mode.

They scatter in different directions, trying to blend in with the Miss Bluebonnet contestants. My heart is racing as my mom walks up to me.

"Hey, Mom," I say casually. *Nuthin' to see here. Move along.*

She gives me this serious, "I'm about to give you a mother / daughter heart-to-heart talk" look, and I pray it will be a quick one.

"Honeybunch, I just wanted to give you a good-luck gift for your big night," she says. Then she hands me a bag, a heavy grocery sack that is a real departure from the Brooke Cavendar style of gift-wrapping. I open the bag and pull out—*no way!*—my skates.

My skates, my skates, my skates, my skates, my skates, my skates!

"Now, let's get out of here," she adds.

"Excuse me?" I say.

"Shania's a natural. She'll be Miss Bluebonnet some-day. But you—you're Babe Ruthless. And you've got a championship to win."

It occurs to me she's not only giving me my skates, but my freedom. I feel my eyes welling with grateful tears. Mom, not missing a beat, takes a visual lap around the dressing room and says, "Which one of y'all came up with that name, anyway?"

Malice's tattooed arm sloooowly rises from behind a rack of frilly dresses as she steps out.

"Clever," my mom says. "But I don't wanna see it tattooed on her arm."

"Done," Malice says, before hugging her and shouting, "Thanks, Mom!"

Subsequent conversations will reveal that Earl was the one who went to war on my behalf. I'm not sure if he blackmailed her, put her in a headlock, or threatened to riot in the streets, but whatever he did, it worked. And that means more to me than anything that happens in the game.

And yes, mad props to Brooke for freeing me from the Miss Bluebonnet cage. It couldn't have been easy for her to turn over those keys.

U Is For . . .

$\mathcal{I}$n what must be the quickest fortune reversal in our little league history, an hour later I am dressed in my Hurl Scouts uniform ready to go. I convince my girls to keep news of my return to the team a surprise.

"C'mon, we won't tell anyone until the skate-out. Then Atom Bomb will announce my name," I say, warming them to the idea.

"Yeah, everyone will freak the fuck out!" Emma adds, backing me up.

So, here we are, in our season championships with the Hurl Scouts facing off against the still-undefeated Holy Rollers. (Which I find boring at this point. *Yay, you. You won again, whoopty-freakin'-do.*) Everybody expects the Rollers to skate to victory without so much as a rip in their new fishnets.

Well, the great thing about life—as I am learning—is the unexpected stuff that happens along the way, and when Atom Bomb announces me last, the crowd really does go bonkers.

Ahhh. It's good to be back, but it's even better to see Dinah's shocked expression. I smile as I watch her inner gears start to malfunction and a little puff of angry smoke comes out of her helmet.

It's the you-got-served moment of the century, and I would be lying if I said I didn't love every second of it.

From the infield, I catch sight of my family in the stands, wedged between a pack of burly rockabilly dudes with tattoo sleeves. Brooke looks hilariously terrified as she tightly holds Shania on her lap. Earl looks around, a little confused, like he's waiting for instructions on how to behave.

It strikes me that if only I had a camera, this would be a perfect Cavendar family Christmas card, not that I'm in charge of those things. But it would be genius.

Razor blows the whistle, and the game is on.

Of course, I haven't skated in two weeks, and it takes a couple of jams to shake off the dust, so Dinah and the Holy Rollers jump out to lead 11 to 6.

Their fans waste no time showing their support, shouting "Roll-ers! Roll-ers!"

But you know what? I did not lie to my parents, create a secret life, and run away from home just to have Dinah Might steal the stage on the one night my family gets to see what it is I turned myself upside down for. They may not be getting Miss Bluebonnet, but they are sure as hell gonna get a show from Babe Ruthless. And it starts now!

The next jam, I sneak right between the Holy Rollers' Robin Graves's legs to get through the pack. When I come back around the track to score, Emma balances on one leg, and I take a Texas-sized whip off her other leg that sends me flying to the outside, past all the Holy Rollers.

And we do it again and again and again, taking the lead. The crowd's chant morphs from "Roll-ers! Roll-ers!" to "Ruth-less! Ruth-less!" The place is electric as everyone gleefully anticipates the Holy Rollers' first loss.

I'm with you, people.

"The Holy Rollers may have God on their side," Atom Bomb shouts from the announcer's booth, "but these Scouts are about to earn their victory badge!"

I look up in the stands and see my mom and Earl and Shania, all standing and screaming. I even see my mom jumping up and high-fiving the burly rockabilly guys. *Now, that's a Christmas card.*

Going into the final jam, the score is Holy Rollers, 34, Hurl Scouts, 38. If Dinah's blockers keep me from scoring, she could easily make up the difference. But that's *if*—I don't care what those naughty schoolgirls have up their dirty little sleeves, I am Not. Going. Down.

Dinah and I line up for the final jam, trading steely stares. She seems awfully confident for someone about to lose, although, upon closer inspection, you can see the psycho-ness brewing in her crazy eyes.

"You can't win, Ruthless," Dinah says coldly.

I smile. "Suck my skate, Dinah."

The whistle blows, and we both take off like rockets, but Dinah cuts me off in the first turn, taking the lead. I push hard, getting all I can out of my hardworking thighs. Malice and Emma go for a wall to slow Dinah, but she ducks and spins between them.

The crowd loves it. I jump over Robin's skate to get out of the pack as Dinah is already halfway around to get her points. *Push, push, push. Just don't give up, don't give up.*

I'm fast, but Dinah's sneaking into the back before me, the crucial three seconds where she can blow past my blockers and get the points before I have a chance to score. *Don't give up, don't give up.*

Dinah cuts high to get around Emma, but Malice throws a Superman diving-block that times perfectly. She wipes Dinah out with such gusto all the other girls go down too.

So I'm flying not into a pack but into a seven-way, Holy Rollers, Hurl Scouts pileup. I close my eyes, say a little prayer, and jump over the wreckage. . . .

. . . And I clear them all! Okay, so I nearly fall on my ass, but I save it with a knee-slide, then regain my standing position. What I lack in style, I make up for in points—four for the Hurl Scouts, zero for the Holy Rollers.

We're all hugging and crying like it's the best moment of our lives. One thing's for sure, seeing a bunch of badass derby girls bawling while their black eyeliner streaks their cheeks is pretty honkin' hilarious.

I won't go on and on and be super-gloaty about the whole thing, but I have to confess, winning the championship is pretty g.d. sweet.

Mom and Dad and Shania run down from the stands and swarm me with hugs.

My dad is beside himself. "Boy howdy, I tell you what, I have seen some ball games in my time, but this right here, that beats all!" Not that Earl would ever say it, but I've always had the feeling he would have loved to have had a football-playing son. I think me playing Roller Derby might be the next best thing.

I turn to my mom, who is clutching her green Hurl Scout pom-pom. "Oh, my goodness, that was so scary!" she squeals, then adds, "I can't wait till next season. I gotta get me a BABE RUTHLESS IS MY BABY T-shirt!"

Shania looks up and says, "Mommy, when can I get some skates?" Brooke responds with an oh-shit look.

As my parents storm the merch table, I find myself briefly alone, observing the scene, letting this whole day wash over me. I know I will revisit it many times for the rest of my life. It's good to have a few of these memories filed away.

And then I hear it—that voice, that familiar voice. "Nice game, sexy," he says. My stomach drops.

I turn, and there _____ is.

"Sorry I didn't get a chance to call. Everything's just been crazy," he says.

I wish I could say that he looks like hell, that he got fat, that he's suddenly been plagued by disfiguring acne. But the truth is, the boy is hot. And nobody rocks a threadbare T-shirt like he does.

For the first time all day, I don't feel strong.

So is this what life is? Even when you have the best day ever—your friends cheer for you, your parents finally understand you (at least for a moment), you accomplish something that you're actually good at—a little spitball of suck has to come flying your way and ruin everything?

I glance at Pash and Bird-man lingering in the background by the track, shoving each other, laughing, and looking completely smitten. A '50s bombshell and the dork who loves her. It's so wrong it's right.

And that's when I realize. With _____, it was so right it was wrong. Too good to be true.

"So are we gonna hang out? Or what?" he asks, flaunting his cool yumminess my way. A quick make-out session is totally tempting, but I know better. I'm a smart girl.

I look him in the eye and answer, "Or what."

Now, I will say this once and once only, and it shall never ever be repeated ever again, but my mom was right.

He does not deserve me. So I turn to go.

"Hey," he says, grabbing my wrist, but I shake free. As I skate away, he is stopped by a wall of my teammates, who suddenly appear to back me up.

"A word of advice," I hear Malice say. "Don't fuck with a girl on skates."

So, I guess I'm supposed to sum up my big Roller Derby adventure with some profound discoveries about what I learned. Yeah, right.

If I have learned anything, it's that life is way more confusing than you think. Your lame parents can have moments of extreme coolness, while the people you think are extremely cool can turn out to be exceedingly lame.

And, honestly, if I can give you one teeny, tiny piece of advice, it is this: Do not date a boy in a band. I repeat, DO NOT DATE A BOY IN A BAND!

But if you insist on blithely ignoring the above wisdom, DO NOT GIVE HIM YOUR BELOVED STRYPER SHIRT. You will never see it again. Trust me. I had to learn the hard way. (And, hell, yes, it still hurts, but it does get better.)

My new & improved quest is to find a guy who is just as music-obsessed as I am but who isn't a musician. I think that's the secret.

So, if you know of any, send 'em my way. Yeehaw.

GOFISH

SHAUNA CROSS

You're a derby doll yourself—is this book at all autobiographical?

A little bit. I grew up in the burbs outside of Austin and spent my preteen years doing the driver's license countdown to freedom. The minute I could get to Austin by myself, I discovered a whole new world.

What made you decide to take up roller derby?

I went to one practice and it was love at first skate. The girls were misfits, but hilarious—a bunch of wild bandits who didn't fit the mold of traditional sports. But, kind and encouraging.

I love that it's a serious sport that doesn't take itself seriously. Plus, roller derby enthusiastically celebrates a very healthy idea of sexuality. You're sexy because you're strong and athletic, not because you're underfed and falling all over yourself to please some boy who totally doesn't even deserve it.

It's like self-esteem camp on skates. With a badass soundtrack. *Muy caliente!*

Bodeen, Texas, is a fictional town. Is it based on a real place?

Kind of. It's loosely based on a small town called Brenham, Texas, home of the regionally famed Blue Bell ice cream (d-lish!). Small towns can be charming, but I think for a lot of teens, they are stifling and boring—especially if you don't fit in.

Your descriptions of pageant life—the pushy mom, the social climbing, the pink suits—are extremely vivid. Do you have firsthand experience?

Just by observation. I never entered the Tiara Olympics myself. I was a competitive ice skater when I was a kid, which has its share of rhinestones and stage moms.

For the record, my own mom is super-rad and not the least bit pushy.

I'm also fascinated by the theme of finding your own identity, discovering who you are—I think it's a really important journey. I'm forever intrigued by parents who try to put an identity on their kids. It's so tragic.

How did you come up with Bliss's derby name? What about your own?

"Babe Ruthless" just seemed to echo who she is—the youngest, but tough.

My skate name is "Maggie Mayhem," but when I thought of "Malice in Wonderland" for the book, I wish I had that one! It was too late to change.

All the other names in the book are kindly on loan to me by the girls who really skate under them. They rule.

 SQUARE FISH

In derby world, your derby name is a big thing. And don't even get me started on the drama that can go down if someone tries to take somebody else's name from another league. Lord have mercy!

Bliss's voice is very colorful in her use of contemporary teen language. How did you manage to capture the tone so accurately?

Um, that's just totally how I talk. Is that a bad thing?

In junior and high school, I was an insane journal keeper, as well as note writer to my friends. (See, kids, back in the day we didn't have texting, MySpace, or Facebook. We had to write our notes *on paper*. The horror!)

Anyway, I decided to write the book as if it were just a really long letter to my BFF.

What did you want to be when you grew up?

Anything creative. One day it was an actress, the next day it was a choreographer. But I was always telling stories, so, eventually, it seemed obvious that I'd be a writer (though I didn't want to admit it for a long time. I thought it seemed boring).

When did you realize you wanted to be a writer?

High school-ish. Film is also a huge part of my life, so I still want to be a director too. And I will.

What's your most embarrassing childhood memory?

I was a chubby kid, so my older brother got the whole neighborhood to call me "Jabba the Hut," or "Jabba" for short. That sucked. But any kind of awkwardness makes you develop in other ways—for me, I became funny. And that has served me well.

Those who have a super-easy life don't usually become the most interesting people.

What's your favorite childhood memory?
Summer nights. All the kids out till midnight or 1 AM playing massive games of hide-and-go-seek. It was epic and innocent.

As a young person, who did you look up to most?
Well, I really searched for cool female role models. And musicians, because I'm such a music nerd.

What was your worst subject in school?
Math. I still don't understand algebraic equations. Why do you have to get the same answer every time? Isn't it more creative to get a different answer each time? It's such a cliché, but I wish I were better at math.

What was your best subject in school?
English. History. I LOVE history and it took me a while to figure out history is more than just "big men and big dates," but also all the day-to-day info about living in different eras. How people survived, who fell in love with whom . . . the little human touches that shape us. I love that stuff. I gobble it up.

What was your first job?
Well, I babysat early on. But my first real job was working for a discount department store called Stein Mart in the accessories department. I had to hang up a lot of belts.

How did you celebrate publishing your first book?
I told my parents; they like stuff like that. And I made my first-ever Barneys purchase. A purse that was waaay on sale. And still crazy expensive.

This is your first published book—tell us about your road to publication.
Well, I've been a semi-successful screenwriter for a coupla years (translation: They pay me to write scripts, but the movies haven't been made yet). On a lark, I thought it would be fun to try writing a novel—just for me.

My awesome friend, and fellow writer, Kirsten Smith, introduced me to Writers House agent Steven Malk.

When I had thirty pages, I sent them to Steve. I was *so nervous* to hear back because, unlike with screenplays, I felt intimately exposed. This book has me all over it.

I never set out to be a "novelist," I didn't go to Bread Loaf or an Ivy League school or have any fancy pedigree that I assume most people in publishing must have. So, it was scary.

But Steve loved the pages and helped get the book sold in a matter of days.

The hilarious irony is that I've worked years to get my screenwriting off the ground, but I stumbled into a publishing career in a matter of months.

However, I am one of those people who take every opportunity thrown my way. Even if I'm scared, I will try something new. Failure is the best learning experience ever. Just like roller derby. Anyone can do it—you just have to be willing to fall on your ass a few (hundred) times. Every once in a while, it really pays off.

Tell us about your writing process. Where do you write? When? What do you eat/drink while you're crafting a story?

I write in my little 1920s apartment in Los Angeles (a cool city that gets a bad rap), which means I live in jam-stained pajamas. Classy.

I wake up, get coffee, crank my stereo (must have music to think), procrastinate by surfing the Web, then get out ye old spiral notebook and handwrite everything before I type it all in.

I never write in public—it makes me feel like a zoo exhibit ("Look, kids! A writer!")—but I do a lot of thinking there. Then I go home and put it on paper.

I try to be healthy, but have been known to binge on Brown Sugar Cinnamon Pop-Tarts in the home stretch of a deadline. Mmmm . . . Pop-Tarts.

Where do you find inspiration for your writing?

Everywhere, everything. I'm a culture vulture, I love all kinds of books, music, movies, people. I think the more varied and vivid your life is, the more you can pull from. Doing things that scare me—getting out of my comfort zone—is a great source of inspiration.

Are you a morning person or a night owl?

I have a baby now, so I'm a forced morning person, but the night owl in me is not happy about it. Not one bit.

What's your idea of the best meal ever?

When you're traveling (like in India or Italy) and you're lost and can barely comprehend the menu, so you guess—and then the

meal is delicious. I love those moments. I love to be pleasantly surprised. Also, exploring divey, hole-in-the-wall joints—there are some good meals to be had in random strip malls.

And some awful ones. You take your chances.

Which do you like better: cats or dogs?
Love them both. I don't like the cats vs. dogs thing. Four legs good, that's all I'm sayin'.

What do you value most in your friends?
Realness. Humor. Loyalty. A sense of adventure. Warmth. Generosity. The ability to forgive and move on. I don't like catty people with agendas; life is way too short.

Where do you go for peace and quiet?
I like to hide out in my bathtub, reading and listening to music. I also love to travel.

What makes you laugh out loud?
A clever twist of words, a witty remark from an otherwise shy person, everyday weird occurrences, and some good physical comedy. I'm a sucker for a pratfall.

What's your favorite song?
There are way too many. But "Paint It Black" by The Rolling Stones, "London Calling" by The Clash, "I'll Be Your Mirror" by The Velvet Underground, "Jolene" by Dolly Parton, "Heavy Metal Drummer" by Wilco, and "Cupid" by Sam Cooke are all damn near perfection. Also "Fox on the Run" by Sweet, "Non, Je Ne

Regrette Rien" by Edith Piaf, "Somewhere Over the Rainbow," "It's Not Easy Being Green," "Cherry Bomb," "Surrender" by Cheap Trick, "Smells Like Teen Spirit," "The KKK Took My Baby Away" by the Ramones.

Who is your favorite fictional character?
Dolly Parton. And Maude from the movie *Harold and Maude*.

What are you most afraid of?
Success going away. It's so fulfilling to get to do what you love and I know I'm incredibly lucky, but I know it may not be forever. Life is short and you have to savor every morsel.

What time of year do you like best?
Early spring, when everything's starting to bloom. And warm summer nights when the days are long—it's so sexy!

What's your favorite TV show?
The Wire is the best thing I've ever seen.

If you were stranded on a desert island, who would you want for company?
I would build my own personal Noah's Arc of kick-ass people, including my close family members, my husband, my son, Dolly Parton, Bea Arthur, and Danny McBride.

If you could travel in time, where would you go?
Paris in the '20s just before the war. Or Cuba in the early '50s—the music! The mojitos!

 SQUARE FISH

What's the best advice you have ever received about writing?

Voice is the most important talent; your individual point of view is what makes something special.

What do you want readers to remember about your books?

I hope they laugh, I hope they feel empowered to do whatever they love.

What would you do if you ever stopped writing?

Interior design.

What do you like best about yourself?

My sense of humor. My quiet confidence. I'm not a boaster because I believe in my talent. I don't have to shut anyone else down to build myself up.

What is your worst habit?

Procrastination. I've tried to work on it, but I keep putting it off. . . . Adulthood is hard!

What do you consider to be your greatest accomplishment?

That I am who I wanted to be when I grew up. I got here on talent and being nice and I think that matters.

Where in the world do you feel most at home?

Well, I live in Los Angeles now, but the being-home feeling is in Austin, Texas, eating tacos, listening to a band, looking at that big, wide sky.

What do you wish you could do better?

Play music. I'm such a fan, but I'm SO not gifted. I've tried. It was not meant to be. And sing. I have the singing voice of a hundred cats dying.

What would your readers be most surprised to learn about you?

I don't know. Maybe that I was a competitive ice-skater as a kid?

Turn the page for a sneak peak at the new movie

WHIP IT